THE GOLD RUSH BRIDE

CYNTHIA WOOLF

STAY CONNECTED!

Newsletter

Want to hear about coming books first?
Sign up for my <u>newsletter</u> and get a free book.

Follow Cynthia

https://facebook.com/CynthiaWoolf
https://twitter.com/CynthiaWoolf
http://cynthiawoolf.com

Don't forget if you love the book, I'd appreciate it if you could leave a review at the retailer you purchased the book from.

Thanks so much,
Cynthia

CHAPTER 1

*J*anuary 1898 – St. Louis, Missouri

KNOCK! Knock! Knock!

Sadie Thompson stopped polishing the banister, the last of her morning chores, and pushed tendrils of red hair back toward the bun from which they escaped. She answered the door and saw, from the uniform the young man wore, he was a Western Union representative.

"Can I help you?"

The young man removed his hat and looked down at the telegram he held. "Miss Sadie Thompson?"

"Yes."

"A telegram for you." He handed her the envelope and then donned his hat.

She took the envelope. "Wait just a moment and I'll get you your tip." She went to the sofa in the living room where she'd left her reticule and got a nickel, then she returned to the door.

"Here you are." She handed the coin to the man.

He tipped his hat. "Thank you, miss."

Sadie closed the door and opened the envelope and read.

YOUR FATHER SUCCUMBED TO INJURIES SUSTAINED IN AN AVALANCHE – STOP – WILL BUY YOU OUT

BARNABY DRAKE

She dropped the telegram and slid down the door to the floor, while tears poured down her face. Dead? Her father was dead? "No!" she screamed. "No, it can't be true." These last words came out in a whisper.

Sadie didn't know how long she stayed that way. She cried until she had no more tears to shed.

What will I do now? She had the house; as she'd inherited it from her grandmother. She'd helped her father raise Sadie when her mother died twenty-five years ago. But she'd been living on the money her father sent each month. Sadie was twenty-seven-years-old and had no appreciable skills to earn a living. Her grandmother taught her how to sew, but working as a seamstress or assistant wouldn't pay enough for her bills. Besides, she didn't want to rent it and be a land-lord, but just the thought of living forever alone in this house that held so many memories didn't appeal to her, either. The following day, she left early and went to her father's best friend and man of business, Angus Murphy. He was a dear man, and her father had trusted him implicitly. He would know what her father's finances were and if they'd struck gold. After all, why else would Mr. Drake want to buy her share of the claim?

She climbed the stairs to the third-floor offices of Jones and Murphy, Esq. Upon entering, she noticed the partners had updated the offices, and a new secretary sat at the desk.

"Good morning, is Mr. Murphy in?" Sadie asked the young, blond man.

"Yes, he is in his office. Please go right in." He pointed at the door to the right of his desk. The door on the left was Mr. Jones's.

Sadie walked into Mr. Murphy's office.

He rose to greet her. His glasses perched on the end of his nose. He combed over silver hair trying, in vain, to cover his bald spot.

"Sadie, my dear, how are you? Please sit." He pointed at one of the leather chairs in front of his desk.

As she sat, she took a deep breath to keep the tears at bay. "I've been better, sir. I received a telegram from a Mr. Barnaby Drake, and I'm here to find out what it means."

"Ah, yes, the telegram. I received one as well. I'm sorry to say it means exactly what it said. An avalanche killed your father. Mr. Drake is...was...your father's partner and wants to buy his share from you."

"Had they hit gold yet? Father sent me money every month, so they must have hit something."

Mr. Murphy shook his head. "I wish I could report that they had, but no, mostly they mined just enough for the three of you to live on."

"Thank you, Mr. Murphy. I really appreciate all you've done."

"It's my pleasure, Sadie. I only wish I could do more."

Sadie thanked him again. She'd hoped the telegram was a mistake, but it wasn't, and she left the office with a heavier heart, knowing it was true. She was now alone in the world, and she wasn't sure what to do. Tears followed a trail down her cheek as she raised her hand and waved it, calling for the Hansom cab.

Inside the cab, she tried to figure out what to do. She knew she had some money, but not enough to live on for more than a couple of months. She'd have to find a job, or perhaps...her mind ran over all the possibilities. Yes. Why couldn't she?

The next morning, Sadie returned to see Mr. Murphy.

"Back so soon?" asked the old man. "Couldn't resist my charms?" He chuckled. But he flashed a warm smile and pointed to the chair in front of his desk.

She sat and faced Mr. Murphy. "Yes, I want to sell the house and anything else father might have left. Everything."

The man's silver brows came together in a deep vee between his eyes. "Are you sure?"

"I'm sure, sir. I want to go to the Klondike and work my father's claim. I really don't have any choice...given my lack of an occupation."

If his jaw had dropped any farther, it would have landed on the desk. "You can't go work the claim. You're a woman."

She huffed a breath. "What has that got to do with anything?"

"Everything. You can't just go off to the Klondike. It's dangerous for men, much less a woman." He shoved an arm in the air. "*Your father was killed there*, for goodness' sake."

Sadie let out a deep breath that ended on a sigh. "Mr. Murphy. There is nothing for me in St. Louis. I have no relatives or even close friends to keep me here. For goodness gracious, I don't even have a pet. Please do as I say and sell everything."

With his mouth in a grim, flat line, he nodded. "As you wish. If you really want to sell, I will buy the house which is your only asset. Your father sold the bonds he had to go on his fool's errand." He pulled a folder from the credenza behind him. "According to my last estimate of the values of your personal investments and the house, your worth is about $2,000.

"The rest of the money is from your grandmother's investments, so that amount could change. It would be challenging for you to survive in that house for over six to eight months with only the investment income, regardless of how frugal you are. However, in that time, you could find someone you want to marry and have children with. Why would you want to risk your life in a wild place like the Klondike?"

"Because I have nothing here. I want to actually live life, not just exist. I can't do that without money. And since I haven't found anyone to marry in twenty-seven-years, it's highly doubtful I'll find anyone in six-months." *I don't count my engagement to Richard. He left me for someone with more money. I just count myself lucky to have found out what men were like before it was too late.* "I have no choice but to go work Daddy's claim. I have no other skills. Besides, I want to do something with my life. Maybe I'll find what I'm looking for. Who knows, maybe the man I'm to marry is there. I'll never know if I don't go."

Mr. Murphy sagged in his chair, took a breath, and then sighed. "Very well. I'll see you have your money as soon as possible. You may remain in your house until you leave. Do you know when that is?"

She shook her head. "I have to read up on what I'll need and then purchase what I can here and the rest when I reach Seattle. I estimate I'll need another month, perhaps less, to accomplish this."

He nodded. "Are you sure I can't talk you out of this, this...fool's errand?"

Sadie smiled at the elderly man. "I'm sure. Thank you for making this as easy on me as possible."

"Of course, m'dear. Your father was my best friend and had been for years. He would first chastise me for letting you go and then would want me to help you in

6

any way I can. Please let me know if I can do anything to aid you."

She rose and extended a hand. "I will. Thank you again." Sadie turned and left with a smile that hadn't been there when she went in." *Klondike, here I come.*

She stopped at the bookstore and found a book called *The Klondike Official Guide* by William Ogilvie. In it, she found lists of things she would need to survive in the Klondike. Canada was not letting people cross their border without a year's worth of supplies or the money to purchase them. This little book was all she needed. She'd buy her clothes here and whatever else she could readily carry. She wasn't getting a tent, or anything like that, because she would live in her father's. She had enough money to purchase food in Seattle or Skagway. But most likely in Seattle because it would be cheaper, and she was more likely to get what she wanted.

The closer she got to leaving, the more she missed her father, and she knew that feeling would never go away.

She'd take the train to Seattle and a steamer to Skagway. Then she would travel over the mountains to Dawson City. That would be the hardest part of the trip. She heard many stories about the men who couldn't make it over the mountain passes and died along the way.

Would that be her fate? To chase a dream and then die before she achieved it? Like her father?

* * *

MARCH 1898

SADIE KNEW she was exceptionally lucky. She could pay to take the new tram over Chilkoot Pass rather than be in the throng of people below her that were having to hike over it. She'd purchased the one-way ticket for her, her horse, Lucky, and the large sled he pulled with all of her goods for a year on it.

She was in awe of the snow-covered mountain peaks rising above as the tram climbed against a stunning blue sky. She placed a hand over her heart. The sight completely and utterly took her breath away.

After the tram ride, she had to ride down the river in one of the many boats going to Dawson City in the Canadian Territory. She'd had to pass a checkpoint where they examined her sled to determine if she had the requisite amount of supplies for a year before she could board the ferry at Lake Bennett. The gold fields were in Canadian Territory, and they were very thorough. They didn't want anyone starving to death.

The boat from Lake Bennett took them down the river through lakes, past forests so thick with trees like maple and pine, you couldn't see into them. She saw one particularly large animal standing in the shallows of one of the smaller lakes. It had an enormous set of antlers.

One boatman came by her.

She stopped him. "Excuse me, sir? Do you know what that animal is?" She pointed to the animal she'd seen.

"That's a moose, ma'am." He tipped his hat and walked on.

"A moose." She giggled. "Now, I've seen everything."

In the lakes, she saw fish jump that were by far the largest she'd ever seen. The lakes were home to waterfowl, but predominantly what she saw were geese.

* * *

LATE MARCH 1898

ARRIVING in Dawson City was an eye-opener. The ramshackle buildings were all wooden, not like the well-built homes and businesses in St. Louis. She saw no streetlights, and macadam wasn't used to pave any of the streets, nor were there concrete sidewalks. All she saw was mud, inches deep in the street, and a few boardwalks in front of some businesses. It appeared to her that they had quickly erected the buildings overnight, using whatever resources were available.

She left Lucky and the sled near the Mountie station, figuring that would be the safest place to leave it. Then she made her way up the street to the Westminster Hotel. Her shoes and the hem of her dress were a mess, but she had few solutions to rectify the situation.

At the front desk, stood a young man with dark hair and a thin build. He wore a shirt that had once probably been white and a dark wool jacket.

"Excuse me."

He looked her up and down. "You're a woman!"

She chuckled. "I am, and I'd like a room for at least one night." She lay her reticule on the counter.

"Yes, ma'am. If you'll just sign the register." He rotated the book toward her and then turned toward the cubby holes behind him and took a key from one." Here you are, room 207." He looked at the registration book and then pointed toward the left of the desk. "Just up those stairs, Miss Thompson."

"Do you know where I might find Mr. Barnaby Drake?"

He grinned. "Everyone knows Barnaby. He'll be down at the El Dorado Saloon, if he's in town."

"Where can I find this saloon?"

"Go out the door and turn right. You can't miss it."

"Thank you." She picked up her carpetbag and headed up to her room.

* * *

LATE MARCH 1898

BARNABY DRAKE STOOD at the saloon's long wood bar. It wasn't the type of mahogany bar found in San Francisco. This one was just a bunch of plywood nailed together and scarcely came to his waist. Of course, they made few places for his height at six feet, four inches. He threw back his head and downed the shot of whiskey. One shot was all he could afford. The prices in Dawson City were outrageous. He would have gotten a room for one night so he could have a hot bath and sleep on a soft bed for the first time in months. The cold baths and sleeping on a cot with no mattress were getting old. But he needed all his money to pay off the Thompson girl. And then get back to the claim along the Klondike River before someone jumped it, and he had to fight them off. He hated claim jumpers. Luckily, they took one look at him and usually changed their minds. He'd had plenty of men who wandered into his camp with the thought of taking it for their own and changed their minds when they saw him.

Now he'd had to leave it to come to this hellhole of a town and meet this woman, just so he could give her the money for the claim. Why he couldn't just wire it, he didn't know.

He turned his head as a ruckus broke out at the entrance to the saloon. He turned to see a woman with bright-red hair enter. What the heck was she doing in here? As if in answer to his question, she spoke.

"I'm looking for Barnaby Drake and was told I could find him here."

Her voice was as pretty as her hair. She'd piled it in curls high on her head, but some rogue tendrils hung around her face.

He turned and pushed his way through the throng of men until he was right in front of the redhead. "I'm Barnaby Drake."

A look of relief flashed through her gaze, replaced by nonchalance. "I'm Sadie Thompson." She held out her right hand. "Pleased to make your acquaintance."

He looked at her hand in amazement. Then he took her by the shoulders. "You shouldn't be in here." He turned her toward the street and guided her out of the saloon, ignoring the jeers and catcalls.

Once outside, he grabbed her arm and steered her away toward the hotel, which was also a brothel. But that couldn't be helped. A lot of businesses in Dawson City were more than one thing, except the general store. They had enough customers without adding another business to their building.

Spring was almost upon them, and the streets ran thick with mud from the snowmelt. He tried to avoid the deepest parts of the street by staying in the ruts made by the horses and mules the miners rode.

"Oh, stop! I'm stuck." Sadie snatched her arm from his hand and tried to balance herself. She teetered backwards, her skirt acting like a sponge in the inch or so of water that covered most of the mud.

He grabbed her hand and pulled her forward. Barnaby realized his mistake when he released her, and she fell...face first, into the mud.

She pushed herself up from the street and looked through slitted eyes. The mud covered her face. Only her eyes and mouth seemed to have been spared.

She sputtered, blowing the mud out of her mouth. "Well, don't just stand there. Help me up."

He might have been mistaken about that. He erupted with laughter as he helped her to her feet.

Once on her feet, she slapped his chest. "Stop laughing at me, you big oaf. This is all your fault. I managed to make it from the Westminster Hotel to the El Dorado Saloon without falling, but you in your efforts to...what? Save my reputation?...You pulled me down the street like I'm some sort of mule."

He sobered and wiped the tears from his eyes. "I'm sorry Miss Thompson. You're right, this is totally my fault. Let me help you." Without another word, he scooped her into his arms and headed toward Kitty's.

She looked up at him with the deepest green eyes he'd ever seen. Fire glittered in her expression. "What do you think you're doing? I'm quite capable of walking at a normal rate of speed."

"Well, I'm not letting you walk in this muck again. You need to get as much of that off before it dries."

He carried her straight to the hotel and didn't set her on her feet until they were inside.

"Here now," said the woman behind the desk. "I get enough of that muck in here without you bathin' in it before you come inside."

"This woman has a room here and needs a bath sent up immediately."

"Those costs extra." The woman eyed Sadie with a critical eye. "Three dollars for the bath in the room."

"Fine," snapped Sadie. "Just add it to my bill and

then send the bath up as soon as possible." She turned and narrowed her eyes at Barnaby. "Will you be here when I'm done? We have some things to discuss."

"I will. We can discuss our business over supper. The Dawson City Restaurant is next door, and it has decent food. This hotel is also a brothel. I just want you to be prepared for what you might see."

"I'll consider myself warned." She drew herself to her full height and headed up to the second floor, trailing mud clot behind her.

Barnaby knew from experience that the rooms for the brothel were on the third floor.

After Sadie left, Barnaby turned to the brunette woman behind the desk. "What was all that cater-wauling about, Kitty? You'd think you'd never had someone show up in that condition and need a bath."

"They've all been men and wanting to be with my girls. No one in that condition is going anywhere near my girls. A little dirt is one thing, but that much mud is a different matter."

"She's not here to see your girls. She's here to see me." Barnaby ground out.

"What kind of business you got with someone like that...her all high-and-mighty in her prissy dress?"

"I couldn't tell. She was wearing a coat. Can you get me a towel or let me wash up in back?"

"Sure. Come on back." She headed down the left hallway toward the kitchen.

Barnaby followed her.

Kitty waited until he'd washed his face and hands.

"You never answered my question, Barnaby. What does she want with you?"

He ran a hand over his face. His dark beard was soft under his fingers. "She's here for some business. She's John's daughter."

Her eyes widened as she grinned and slapped her leg. "Whooeee! John's daughter. I never in a million years would have expected her to be here. Didn't he say she was rich? Been left lots of money from her grandma?"

"So, he said. But if that's so, why is she here?"

CHAPTER 2

*A*fter her bath, Sadie felt much better. Her cheerful countenance had returned. She did, however, feel her mining clothes would be more appropriate for this town rather than her dresses. She'd only brought one dress and one skirt with a blouse with her. But she'd gone against Mr. Ogilvie's directions of the clothing to bring. She packed more of certain items, such as two pairs of wool pants instead of one and two overalls. She also put in six pairs of artic socks and wool socks. She was determined to be as comfortable as possible. Besides, since she didn't have to bring things like a tent, she had more room for clothing in her duffle bag.

She brought all the food, and some of the tools recommended by Mr. Ogilvie's guide. It had to be enough to survive for a year, usually weighing in at around one-thousand pounds. Canada wouldn't let you cross their border without it.

Dressed in a pair of wool pants, she also wore long underwear underneath, for comfort against the itchy wool. She put on a heavy cotton shirt and miner's lace-up boots. She wouldn't have to worry about them coming off in the mud like her half boots could. Then she donned her coat and gloves. Sadie headed downstairs and found Barnaby Drake sitting in the lobby, waiting.

He looked up and his eyes opened wide enough for the eyeballs to pop out.

She walked over. She'd realized he was a big man. When they'd been standing next to each other, she'd had to look up at him, which was unusual since she was five feet ten inches. But he dwarfed the chair he sat in. His hair was the darkest brown, as was his beard, and his midnight blue eyes seemed to bore into her. "These should keep me from falling again." She flashed a smile and twirled in front of him. "Don't you agree?"

He took her arm and pulled her to the side of the room. "What I agree on is if those miners see you, you'll start a stampede. What do you mean, wearing clothes like that?"

"I mean to go to my claim and work it, just like any other miner."

"You can't go into the wilderness alone."

"I won't be alone unless you'll let me buy you out," she countered.

"That. Is. Not. Happening. Ever." He fisted his hands.

The anger on his face almost gave her pause about

17

her idea. But she forged on. "Then what do you propose?"

He was silent for a moment as he pulled his beard to a point on his chin. "There is only one way you can go up there." He stopped and narrowed his eyes. "Are you sure you won't just let me buy you out? It would make things a whole lot easier on everyone."

She tilted her head and lifted her brows, then crossed her arms over her chest. "No, I won't sell. What's the way out?"

"You'll have to marry me. If you're my wife, no one will bother you."

He was testing her, trying to make her turn tail and run. But she wasn't about to. Perhaps a marriage of convenience was just what was called for. She could use his protection. She wasn't stupid and knew what he was saying was true. Having all those men surrounding her at the saloon taught her that. "Very well. When can we do it? I'd like to be on our way as soon as possible."

His mouth formed a thin line.

She lifted a brow, knowing he hadn't expected her to agree, and now he'd have to marry her.

"Today. Here. In one hour. I have to go find the preacher. He doesn't have a church, just goes saloon to saloon and preaches."

"Fine. I'm waiting here so I'm ready when you return."

"Fine." He stomped out of the lobby.

Sadie looked at Kitty. "Is he always so cranky?"

Kitty laughed. "Only on days he gets married."

Shaking her head, Sadie crossed her arms over her chest, then dropped them and sat in the chair Barnaby had vacated. She crossed and uncrossed her knees but couldn't seem to get comfortable.

She jumped up when Barnaby returned around thirty minutes later with a man carrying a Bible and wearing a long black coat. He had the white collar of a reverend. His hair was black and hung stringy around his face, but his face and hands were clean.

He smiled.

Sadie smiled back and relaxed.

"My name is Reverend Calloway. I understand you and Barnaby are getting married. You can't imagine how happy that makes me. I'd love to see other couples do the same, but..." He sighed. "Women are in short supply here."

"Which is why we're getting married," growled Barnaby.

Reverend Calloway chuckled. "So, you are. Are you both ready?"

"Yes, Reverend." Sadie smiled at the man of God.

"Yes." Barnaby frowned.

She was sure he didn't see anything in this whole situation to smile about.

"Now, before I get started, are there rings to exchange?"

"No," Barnaby and Sadie spoke at once.

"That's fine. I'll just skip that part of the ceremony. Do you have two witnesses?" The reverend opened his Bible and waited.

Sadie wondered if she was doing the right thing.

* * *

Barnaby looked around. "Kitty, can you get one of your girls and the two of you be our witnesses?"

"Sure. Hang on." She disappeared behind a curtain in the back wall of the lobby. She returned shortly with a tall, plump brunette. Barnaby couldn't help but stare. The woman had a lot of Sadie's attributes, but none of her fire. Perhaps Sadie's bright-red hair or her emerald eyes made her appear livelier than the other woman. Or maybe she'd just had a hard life.

"This here's Janey." Kitty pointed her thumb toward the woman. "She's one of my new girls. I don't think you've met her, Barnaby."

His cheeks heated under Sadie's scrutiny. "No, I've never had the pleasure. Nice to meet you, Janey."

The woman extended her right hand. "You too, Barnaby. Who is the lucky lady?"

He leaned toward Janey and shook hands.

Smiling while she stepped forward, Sadie extended her right hand. "I'm Sadie. I just arrived here today."

Janey wore a woolen shawl over her dress. She also wore woolen stockings with miner's boots and a dress that was shockingly scandalous. It hit her just above the knees in front and mid-calf in back. While the shawl covered most of Janey's dress, he saw Sadie still discerned it to be a too low-cut dress. Barnaby wished he'd asked Kitty to have her girl put on a Sunday dress.

The reverend gazed down at his Bible and then back and forth toward each of them. "Now that everyone has met, shall we get started?"

Barnaby straightened and stood to the reverend's left.

Sadie positioned herself to his right.

"Very good. Now your names, please."

"Sadie Aurora Thompson."

"Barnaby Samuel Drake."

"Good. Let's begin. We are gathered here before God and these witnesses for the marriage of Barnaby Samuel Drake and Sadie Aurora Thompson. Do you, Barnaby Samuel Drake, take this woman Sadie Aurora Thompson, to be your lawful wedded wife? To have and to hold, for better or for worse, in sickness and in health, for richer and for poorer, to love and to cherish her from this day forward, until death do you part?"

He gazed at Sadie for a moment and then nodded. "I do."

The reverend turned toward Sadie. "Do you, Sadie Aurora Thompson, take this man, Barnaby Samuel Drake, to be your lawfully wedded husband? To have and to hold, for better and for worse, in sickness and in health, for richer and for poorer, to love and to obey him from this day forward, until death do you part?"

"I do." Her voice was soft.

She looked up at Barnaby with those beautiful green eyes and he thought maybe this wasn't such a bad idea.

The preacher smiled. "Then by the power vested in

me by the Lord God Almighty, I now pronounce you man and wife. You may kiss your bride."

Barnaby looked down at Sadie. She was a beautiful woman, and when, like now, she was quiet, he wanted to kiss her...very much. He bent his head and placed his lips on hers. He meant it to just be a quick peck, but her lips were soft, and he found himself wanting to drink in all her goodness.

He placed one hand behind her head and kissed her thoroughly until he felt a tap on his shoulder.

"Mr. Drake. Mr. Drake." The preacher continued to tap his shoulder.

Barnaby wanted to turn and growl at the man as he lifted him into the air with one hand. But he didn't do it. He ended the kiss and leaned back.

Sadie had her eyes closed and her lips pursed like she was waiting for another kiss.

He might have to explore more of that later. But for now, he was hungry and wanted to keep Sadie off the street as much as possible. Looking like she did, even being married to him wouldn't save her from some men.

"Let's get something to eat and we can talk, now that you're safer."

"Surely, no one will challenge you. Isn't that why we did this?"

He stiffened his spine and dropped his chin. "We got married to protect you, but with some men, that won't be enough. In case you didn't know it, *Mrs. Drake*, not all men are good, upstanding citizens."

She put her hands on her hips and lifted her chin. "I'm well aware of that, *Mr. Drake* and I would never have gone through with this...this—"

"Marriage is the word you're looking for." He lifted a brow and smiled.

She stamped a booted foot. "Yes," she said between clenched teeth. "This marriage, if I didn't believe you were a good man. My father wouldn't have been partners with a miscreant. And I know it won't stop all men, but most men are respectful of a man's wife."

"If you weren't so determined to work the claim, if you'd let me buy—"

Her fiery eyes were directed at him. "I'm not selling. Period."

"I don't know what it is you expect to find."

"I want to understand what my father found that kept him from me for so long. What was he seeking that he couldn't find with me in St. Louis?" She bit her lower lip and then soothed it with her tongue.

Barnaby watched and, for the life of him, he wished he was the one to soothe that lip. He closed his eyes and gave himself a mental shake. "Maybe he wanted something of his own. Maybe he didn't want you to support him. I know you're wealthy because your maternal grandmother left you everything. Maybe he thought that living off of you wasn't what he wanted for his life. He wanted more. He aspired to be independent."

She let out a single laugh. "I'm not wealthy. Daddy thought Grandma had much more money than she did, but I was living off what he sent me every month. Grandma left me the house and some bonds worth about five-hundred dollars. I cashed them in and sold the house to come here. And why would it be okay for me to live off of him? I'm a grown woman."

They'd kept their coats on for the marriage cere-mony, so headed directly out onto the boardwalk.

He nodded as they walked next door to the restau-rant. "And yet you did. Don't you see? You're his daughter. Society expects it to be that way, at least until you marry. Then it is your husband's responsibility to take care of you. Even though he thought you were wealthy, he still sent you money...to support you...be-cause that's what a father does."

"I don't desire to be anyone's responsibility."

He lifted an arm to signal the waitress. "Too bad. That's the way of the world, and the sooner you accept it, the better."

She crossed her arms over her chest. "Hmpft."

The waitress appeared.

Her disheveled appearance showed how busy the place was. Of course, it was dinnertime, and Barnaby's stomach growled with hunger. He hadn't eaten lunch, and he was now starving. Someone was always awake, regardless of the time of day or night. So, some busi-nesses, like the saloons and the restaurants, were open twenty-four hours a day.

Barnaby held up two fingers. "Table for two."

She was a blonde. It appeared half her hair had come out of her bun and hung in sweaty curls around her face and neck. "This way." She pointed toward the back wall. "Menu's there. I hope you don't mind sitting by the window. It's the only table we have open."

"That's fine."

He put his hand on Sadie's waist and guided her as they followed the woman. She showed them to a table for two right in front of the window. Shortly, a group of men gathered outside the window fixated on Sadie.

Barnaby looked out the window and saw a group of about twenty men had gathered outside on the board-walk. They were jostling and pushing to get closer to the window. He pointed. "Now, do you understand why you need a husband? If you don't, then head outside without me."

She looked again at the throng of men. "No, thank you. I'll pass on that."

Barnaby chuckled and set his hat on the back of his chair. "Believe me now?"

She nodded. "You were right." She looked him in the eye and lifted a brow. "But that doesn't mean you always will be."

A petite brunette woman came to the table. "What'll it be?"

Sadie looked at the board. "I'll have the stew and bread with butter if you have it."

"Got it, one stew." She smiled at Barnaby. "And what about you, Barnaby?"

"I'll have the same, but double portions. You know what I like, Edie."

"That I do, sugar. That I do." She chuckled and tilted her head toward Sadie. "Who's she?"

He gazed at Sadie. "She's John's daughter...and...my wife."

Her eyes widened. "Your...wife?"

"That's right. We got married this morning."

"You could have said something last night," she screeched, her hands on her hips and her eyes narrowed.

Sadie, face flaming, closed her eyes and covered her face with a hand.

"I didn't know last night. If I had, we wouldn't have had a last night." Barnaby glanced around and kept his voice low. "It's only because she wants to work her daddy's claim, and I can't have an unmarried female up there."

Edie took a deep breath, placed her hands at her sides, and looked at Sadie. "Is that right? This is only for show?"

Sadie nodded. "Only for show. I needed protection when I'm out there and this was the way to do it. No one can question a man's wife helping him work the claim."

The brunette put an index finger on her chin. "Yeah, I guess that makes sense. When are you all headed back?"

"Tomorrow morning at first light," said Barnaby.

"So, does that mean we can see each other tonight?" She winked at him.

He shook his head. Niggling in the back of his mind

was a smidgen of guilt for letting Edie talk about sex in front of Sadie...after all, she was his wife, even if in name only. But he couldn't fault Edie either. "I can't. If it got out that I didn't spend my wedding night with my bride, then everyone would know about the marriage."

Edie sighed. "Yeah, that would sort of give it away. Then I'll see you next time you come to town, if I'm still here."

Barnaby reached out and ran his finger down her cheek. "I'll see you then."

"Okay." Edie put her pad and pencil in her apron pocket. "Three stews coming up with coffee." She turned and headed back to the kitchen.

"I'm sorry." She looked down at the table. "I didn't know this would affect you so. It never occurred to me you might have a sweetheart."

Barnaby chortled. "Edie isn't my sweetheart. She works in the brothel next door at night and here in the afternoons until just after dinner. Then she goes back next door."

"Oh." Sadie's eyes were wide.

Barnaby was sure she was curious. "Do you want to know what the women in the brothel do?"

She closed her eyes and shook her head. "No. Yes. No. It's unnecessary. I assume they have sex for money."

"That would be correct. All of them except Kitty. She's retired from that and is now the madam. She only hires women willing to work at both the brothel and

27

the restaurant because we have a shortage of women, in case you didn't know."

She laughed.

Apparently, he was entertaining. He liked the sound of her laugh. It wasn't a belly laugh but was deep and rich. She didn't titter. And the way her eyes sparkled like the finest emerald...he could look at that forever. If they could find amusement with each other, it would bode them well when winter came.

"I figured out that they were in short supply by the reaction of the men to me. I've never caused a scene like that before."

They were quiet for a few minutes before he spoke again.

"There is something we need to discuss."

She rested her forearms on the table and then clasped her hands. "What would that be?"

"Our wedding night."

She reared back in her chair. "What? Wedding night? What do you mean?"

CHAPTER 3

Sadie tried to calm herself but was having difficulty. She fisted and unfisted her hands, wishing Barnaby's neck was between them. "We are not having a *wedding night*," she hissed. "We are married in name only."

"Will you keep your voice down?" He frowned and looked around.

Her gaze darted around the room. No one seemed to pay attention. She leaned forward. "We are not having a wedding night. Period."

"Look. We'll head out as soon as possible after breakfast, but in the meantime, you have a room for the night and I mean to stay in it, as your husband. You can have the bed. I'll take the floor. At least it'll be warmer than usual."

"I intend to take over my father's lodgings when we get to our claim."

He threw his head back and laughed. "Just what do you think your father's lodgings comprise?"

"Well, I assume there is a tent and a cot with blankets, perhaps a fur for warmth."

Barnaby shook his head. "We shared one tent, though there are separate cots. When we started out, we tried to save as much weight as possible. With only our two backs and hand sleds, it limited how much we could carry. We brought what we could to Dawson City and then went back to the Scales on the other side of Chilkoot Pass for the supplies we had to leave behind." He leaned forward and placed his head as close to her as he could. "That's five-hundred miles each way. You were lucky, Sadie. They have the tram now and I assume you had enough money to pay the fare. As you know, you can't cross into Canada without one year's provisions or the money to buy them. That's two-hundred dollars. How many of those men do you figure had that kind of money to throw away? Only a few."

She nodded, but whispered. "I'd have given him the money."

"Don't you get it? He didn't want your money. That's why he was here."

She stiffened her back. "I took the tram, and I have a horse and a sled. So, what? And, yes, it's true about Canada, and I made sure to have the proper amounts of everything according to their list. So, what? You have one tent, one stove. What else?"

"We had one set of pots and pans, one hatchet, one whip saw, an axe, well, you get the idea."

"Yes, so we'll have to share. I have no problem with that and with my fresh supplies, you will probably have better meals than what you're used to of late."

The waitress returned with their meals. "Here you are." She set them on the table along with a loaf of bread. "Enjoy." She hurried to the next table to take their order.

Barnaby broke off a piece of bread and took a bite.

Sadie followed suit. The bread had a unique, kind of tangy flavor but was very enjoyable. "What is this? It's good, but I don't recognize the flavor."

He dipped a chunk in the stew.

She figured that was because she saw no butter. "I guess I shouldn't ask, but is there butter?" This was all so different from home. She'd never been without. Their table had always had butter and everything else she wanted. Even without her mother, her father had seen to her needs. She missed her father. Even though he'd been gone from her physically, she always knew he was alive and that he would be returning to her. Now, he never would. Tears filled her eyes. She had to close them before the tears rolled down her cheeks and she'd sob.

"Did you see any cows on your way here or after you arrived?"

Realizing Barnaby was talking to her about the missing butter, she sniffled. "No."

"Then you have your answer. They can bring butter

in, but it's ten-dollars or more a pound. It's not worth the weight to carry it over the pass or pay the tram fee for it. As to this," he held up his piece of bread. "It's sourdough. It doesn't need yeast and you can keep the starter for years, if needed. You just feed it every once a week or after each use."

"Feed it?" *What could he mean? Feed it like an animal?*

He nodded. "Just add some flour and water to the starter and it will last forever. At least ours has." He took a bite of the gravy soaked bread.

She lifted her brows and tore off another chunk of bread. "Ours? You bake?"

He shook his head and barked out a laugh. "Not me. Your dad."

"Really? Daddy baked?." She looked at the bread. "Sourdough. Interesting. I quite like it."

"Good, because other than biscuits, it's the only bread you'll have here."

She nodded and dunked her bread like he'd done. The stew was flavorful, with a rich broth and potatoes and a few chunks of onion. Once she'd swallowed, she pointed at the stew. "This is very good. I know it's not beef. What is it?"

"Elk. Good eating if you can shoot one and drop it immediately. Having to chase a wounded animal is difficult and it can sometimes go for miles before it dies."

"Why? What difference does it make? You'd have to walk longer."

He shook his head. "No. You don't understand. I

have to clean, skin, and cut as much meat as I can carry. And then walk home in dangerous territory with many predators and raw meat on my back."

Her eyes opened wide. "I didn't know it was so involved. I thought you could just drag the animal back to camp."

Barnaby chuckled and wiped his mouth with his napkin. "Elk are as big as a horse and can weigh up to two-thousand pounds for a large bull with a big rack."

She took another bite of the stew. The flavor was exquisite. "What's a rack? And what do you consider a big rack?"

Barnaby set his spoon into one of his empty bowls and reached for more bread. "The rack are their horns. I saw a seven-point royal once. It was gorgeous, seven points on each side. The points are where the horns jut out, kind of like branches on a tree." He took a hand and separated the fingers. "I estimated the rack probably weighed about two hundred pounds alone."

Sadie looked at her own half-full bowl. She could never finish it all. "Would you care for the rest of my stew? I'm full."

He smiled. "Yes, please."

She exchanged her bowl for his.

Barnaby pulled off another piece of bread and dunked it into the stew. The gravy dripped onto his beard. He took his napkin and wiped it off before digging into the savory dish again.

When he was done, he leaned back and patted his flat belly. "Thank you. I'm actually full for the first time in a long while. Once we get back to the camp, we will be much more conservative with our supplies."

"When will we leave for the camp? At first light, you said. What time is that?"

"They serve breakfast around five tomorrow morning. We'll leave about six. We're still in Canadian territory, so at least there are no borders to cross. But we'll be walking and the claim is about twenty miles from here, so it will take us most of the day to reach it."

"My supplies are on a sled at the Mounties' office with my horse, Lucky. I figured they would be safe there. I was fortunate I could take the tram over the pass. I packed grain for Lucky, but the trip took longer than I expected and even with the tram, it was difficult."

"Your supplies should be fine. You're fortunate with the horse. John and I also had a horse, but it died before reaching the river on the second trip to retrieve our supplies."

Sadie looked outside. Thankfully, the men had departed. Perhaps they had tired of staring at her. It surprised her to see light still shone on the building across the street. It was past eight o'clock at night since they were late starting because of all that had happened since she arrived. She'd never get used to this. "Is it light here all the time?"

"Nah. In the winter, it's dark about eighteen to twenty hours a day. The other hours don't get very sunny, mostly just an orange glow, though sometimes it can be purple. Winter is very hard here." He shot her a narrow look. "Are you sure you want to stay? You could go back right now if you wanted."

She lifted a brow. "I'm staying. I've got nothing in Missouri. No family, no friends, no pets. Nothing. I don't want to go back to that. I might make friends here, and look...I've already gotten married." She laughed.

Barnaby growled. "That's not funny. And wouldn't have been necessary if you possessed a lick of common sense."

She frowned. He stole her good humor. "Well, now, I have you for that, don't I?"

He shook his head and rolled his eyes. "Let's get out of here. I'm tired and want to get some sleep before we start out." He left money on the table for their bill, stood and donned his hat.

Sadie stood, too, and started for the door.

Barnaby placed his hand at her waist and guided her out.

She walked down the boardwalk toward the Mounties' office. She flipped up her collar and pulled her coat tighter around her. "It's cold."

"This is nothing. Wait until it's winter. Then you'll see what real cold is like."

She shivered. "What time is sunset?"

Barnaby put his arm out for her. "About ten-thirty at night. We have what seems like endless days for a while. And then, in winter, we have what seems like endless nights, with sunrise at about noon and sunset at about four-thirty. Then we'll work into the night because the days are so short."

She placed her hand through the crook of his elbow, despite the mud that was still on him from when he carried her. *He's such a gentleman. After the mob earlier, I hadn't expected this sort of civility.*

"I'm not afraid of hard work. I plan on keeping up my share of the bargain."

"Good, because I don't plan on doing the work for two and having you lying about in the tent all day."

She looked up at him as her brows screwed lower. "I would never do that."

"What about when you're pregnant?"

Her face burned. "That will not happen," she whispered, "and you already know why." *This is not a topic that is usually raised in mixed company. Is he trying to shock me?*

Barnaby shrugged. "Sometimes, things change."

"Well, they are not about to change for us. Ours is a business arrangement. Nothing more." She waited for him to say something.

But he didn't, just kept walking.

"Will you teach me how to shoot? I bought a rifle and a pistol, with plenty of ammunition for both. I also brought my father's old shotgun, which I already know how to shoot."

He nodded. "I'll teach you because you must know, and we'll need a lot of ammo to teach you. But I'd rather not use it all, because we'll need some for hunting and protection, so I hope you are a quick learner. We have to be vigilant. There are claim jumpers who are always trying to take over a working claim."

They walked into the hotel, and Sadie led the way to her room. She took the key from her pocket and opened the door. The room was comfortable looking. An old iron bedstead, a chair, and a chest of drawers were the only things present.

"I'll ask for some extra blankets, and I'll sleep on the floor."

Sadie rubbed her gloved hands up and down her arms. Then bit her lower lip. "Very well."

Barnaby left to get the extra blankets.

When he returned, he made a pallet for himself on the floor.

Sadie sat on one side of the bed and removed her boots. The mud that hadn't flaked off while they walked still caked them. It came off in chunks, even as she removed them. Fortunately, she'd tucked her pants in the boots so she wouldn't soil the bed.

Once her boots were off, she lay back and sighed. "I can't believe how bone tired I am." As if to punctuate her sentence, she yawned wide. "Sorry. I know I'll be a lot more tired up at the claim, but I can't help but yawn now." She closed her eyes and turned her back toward Barnaby, where he lay on the floor.

She lay there for a while. Guilt filled her for making him sleep on the floor. But she'd never had a man in her bed, still he was her husband and they were both adults. *I wonder what it would be like to sleep next to a man. Will I enjoy waking up next to him?*

She turned over in the bed and looked down at Barnaby. "If you want, I could sleep under the sheet and you on top of it. Then we'd both stay warm. It's freezing in here. There's not a fireplace and you'll be cold if you sleep on the floor."

Barnaby lifted a brow. "You'd do that for me?"

She stiffened her back. "We'll be living together. If I thought you were anything but a gentleman, I wouldn't have agreed to the arrangement."

Barnaby took off his hat. "That's very kind of you, Sadie. I would like very much to sleep on the bed. At the camp, you'll find that the cots are not that comfortable or that warm, but it is what it is. John and I did our best to make the place comfortable."

"I'm sure you did, and I'll be fine. You'll see. I'm very adaptable," she grinned. "When I want to be. Besides, I brought more blankets. Maybe that will help some."

"Extra blankets are always welcome."

Sadie turned her back to him and was asleep within minutes.

* * *

BARNABY QUIETLY CHUCKLED. His *wife* snored. And not some soft little whimper. She snored, just like her father had...great sawing sounds came from the other side of the bed. He didn't know if it was a coincidence or a family trait, but he'd already gotten used to her father's snores, so hers didn't bother him. He turned his back to her and closed his eyes...a smile tugging at his lips.

* * *

SADIE AWOKE and her eyes widened as she realized she'd cuddled next to Barnaby, and her arm lay across his chest. She lifted her arm and tried to roll over away from him.

He chuckled. "Finally awake I see."

She pulled her arm back and scrambled from the bed. "I'm sorry. I must have gotten cold during the night."

"It's okay." He sat up, swinging his long legs over the side of the bed. "It's early, but it's better for us to get an early start. Usually, I don't have any problem getting up, but today I would have slept in. I enjoyed sleeping in a proper bed. Thank you again."

"You're welcome." *It was so nice waking up next to him. I wonder if I'll ever get to wake up next to him again? And do I actually want to? After all, I'm the one who insists this is not a genuine marriage. Do I want it to be?*

* * *

WHILE TREKKING up the Klondike River, Sadie saw some of the most beautiful country she'd ever seen. Snow still covered a lot of the ground, but as it melted, tiny rivers flowed toward the large one. In many places, the river slowed to a crawl and little ponds formed. The water was calm enough that she saw fish jump, their rainbow colors sparkling in the sunshine before they splashed back into the pond.

After walking for more than half the day, Sadie was exhausted by the time they got to the claim. However, rest was not to be had. A claim jumper was there. The man had a tall stature, dirty blond hair, and a long, untrimmed beard. He was skinny and coming out of their tent. She saw he was holding the sweater she'd knitted for her father before he left for the gold fields. She fisted her hands. "He's got my father's sweater," she said. Suddenly, her father's death was even more real. He wouldn't have left her gift to him behind if he'd known he wouldn't be back. Her heart was in her throat or she would have sobbed.

"Homer Grimes. I see you. What have you poached from me? Just for jumping my claim, I could kill you. And I probably should, so you don't do this to somebody else," Barnaby shouted as he stomped toward the claim jumper.

Homer Grimes stopped and looked at Sadie, then he dropped the sweater and ran.

Barnaby gave chase and started sprinting after the man but stopped abruptly and walked back to Sadie.

After Homer was gone, she pulled Lucky to the claim and tied his lead rope to a tree. She hurried to the tent and picked up her father's sweater from the ground and clutched it to her chest. Sadie entered the tent and sat on a cot, crying. She missed him so much.

She set the sweater onto the cot and, despite her exhaustion, she helped Barnaby unpack Lucky and the sled.

Barnaby placed the supplies onto a tarp and covered them with another, which he tied down with stakes that were already in the ground. She knew the ground was too hard right now, so he or her father must have done it in the summer when the ground had thawed some.

"I've marked the boundaries of our claim and strung a rope between the marker sticks. Don't go out of our claim."

"All right. I'll pay attention."

The tent was quite large, big enough for two men. Her father had been six feet tall, but slender, unlike Barnaby, who was at least four inches taller and muscular. She hadn't paid any attention when she was in it before, other than the two cots. In the middle of the tent, along one wall, was the stove. The pipe went through a square of tin and then out the top of the tent. Next to the stove were neat stacks of firewood and kindling.

At the back of the tent was a small square table with two chairs. That was it. It appeared each man had personal items in a metal locker under his cot. *Are Daddy's belongings still in the locker under his cot?*

To the east of the camp, there appeared to be a fireplace dug into the hillside with a long table across from it. *Why would they have had a fireplace outside when they had the stove inside?*

"Barnaby, which cot was my father's?"

"The one where you put the sweater. I thought you knew."

"No, I just set it down. Does the locker still contain his clothing?"

"It does. But I don't think you'll find much that is useable. The only thing he had of use was that sweater." He pointed at the clothing next to her on the cot. "He didn't wear it unless we went to town. He'd clean up, put on his best shirt and that sweater."

She picked up the sweater again and buried her face in it, hoping she could still smell him...the sandalwood scent he always wore. It remained...faint, yet present. She held it to her face, and she cried.

Barnaby came and sat next to her. He put an arm around her shoulders and eased her body into his. Then he just held her. He couldn't do anything else, but she was so glad he tried.

When she had regained her composure, she sat up. "Thank you. I just miss him."

"I understand. I do, too. John was my friend as well as my partner. We shared a lot. Now, why don't you rest a bit. I'll just do a bit of fishing and see if I can catch our supper.

Sadie lay down on her father's cot, pulled a blanket over herself and slept with her head on the sweater.

She didn't know how long she slept before she felt Barnaby shaking her by the shoulder.

"Wake up. It'll be time to eat soon."

She blinked several times. "Barnaby?"

"Yes, now wake up. Get up."

Sadie sat up and rubbed the sleep from her eyes. She sniffed the air. "What is that? It smells great."

He grinned and pointed to the pan on the stove. "Fish. I got lucky and caught some good-sized ones. We'll eat well tonight."

"What can I do?" She smoothed back her hair from her face.

He nodded his head toward the table. "Sit. We have fried fish and mashed potatoes."

Barnaby served up the fish, putting a whole fish on her plate.

He put two fish on his plate and started another batch to fry. He put the pan back on the stove.

"How did you fry them? I like it."

"I rolled them in cornmeal and fried them in lard until they were crisp on the edges."

She took another bite. "What kind of fish is this?"

"This is grayling. It's good eating."

"Grayling. It reminds me a little of a trout Daddy caught once when he took me camping. But I don't remember what it tasted like."

"Trout is similar. They are in the same family and both are a good fish for food." He cut his up the back on both sides of the spine and gently released the meat from the bones.

Sadie watched him and tried to do the same, but she still had the small bones to remove from her mouth before she swallowed them.

After dinner, Barnaby heated water for the dishes. "I

don't do this often, but when I've had fish, it flavors everything after it if I don't clean them well. If you want to wash your face before the dishes, now is the time to do it, before it gets too hot. You'll find washcloths and towels in your father's things if you need them."

She glanced down at the locker, not yet ready to open it. "Thanks, but I've got some of my own." She opened one of her duffle bags and found the washcloths and towels on top.

After washing her face and hands, she took the dishtowel from Barnaby and dried the dishes while he washed them in the hot water and rinsed them in cold.

When they were done, she got the extra blankets from the duffle with the washcloths. She gave him two and kept two.

She prepared for bed, taking off her coat and boots but leaving everything else on.

Barnaby pointed at her head. "You should put on a wool stocking cap."

"Why?"

"It will help you stay warmer."

"I've got lots of thick hair. That should keep me warm enough."

Barnaby shrugged. "Do as you please." He pulled on a stocking cap. "Thank you for the blankets." He folded each one in half and laid them on the cot and then placed one unfolded blanket over the top to keep them in place.

Sadie watched and did the same.

"Barnaby, what if the claim jumper comes back in the night?"

He barked out a laugh. "Homer come anywhere near a camp with people in it? He's too much of a coward to do that. You're perfectly safe. Go to sleep." He turned his back to her.

She climbed beneath her covers and wondered what it will be like sleeping in the same space as Barnaby night after night. Will she always feel this reticence? Would she always worry that maybe she'd made a mistake coming here? What was she honestly doing here? Was it to find her fortune or to find what her father saw that kept him away from her?

* * *

SADIE AWOKE before the sun came up. She should have worn the wool cap like Barnaby had suggested. The couple of extra blankets helped, but she was still cold.

Barnaby was still sleeping.

She slipped out of the tent to do her business and was sorry she did, but didn't have any choice. Barnaby had showed her the pit, back away from the camp and the river, in the trees. They'd made it with a log over it so the user could sit.

When she returned, she lit their wood-burning stove and put the coffee pot on it to heat. It still had frozen coffee inside it, but the liquid would thaw...eventually.

He awoke as the coffee scented the tent with its aroma. "That smells good."

"Would you like some coffee? I think it's hot now."

He pushed back his blankets and swung his legs over the side of the cot. "I would. I'll be right back." He put on his coat and left for a bit.

She took six strips of bacon and put them in a pan to fry. Then she found the Lamont's crystallized eggs she'd purchased on a whim and mixed them with water until they were the consistency of beaten eggs. She waited for the coffee to finish heating and then removed the pot from the stove and set another skillet in its place. She waited until the bacon was almost done before starting the eggs.

"Barnaby?"

"Hmm?" he responded, even though he was just drinking his coffee.

"Why is it taking so long for the bacon to cook? It should be done by now."

He sat at the table and leaned back in his chair. "We're at a higher altitude than St. Louis, so it takes longer for the water to boil and food to cook. You'll get used to it."

She lifted a brow. "I don't expect to be preparing all our meals once I'm working mining for gold. Will you teach me how to do that today?"

He shook his head. "Nope. We need to teach you to shoot today. That's the most important thing right now. You have to protect yourself against predators, both the four-legged and the two-legged variety."

I never expected to have to guard myself against other miners. "Are there many men so desperate that they would try to take another's claim, like that man yesterday?"

"They aren't desperate so much as lazy. They don't want to work for anything if they can help it. That's why you need to protect yourself." He sipped his coffee. "They will kill you if you give them the opportunity. So we'll do our best to make sure they never get the chance."

Her eyes widened. Suddenly, the danger she was aware of was actually there. Her stomach roiled. "Very well. I shall learn how to shoot the rifle and the pistol."

Barnaby nodded. "For close up, the shotgun is an excellent choice. Just point and pull the trigger. No need to aim."

Sadie took a bite of the eggs. They were actually good. She wouldn't mind eating these at all. She thought about the lessons today and swallowed the lump in her throat. Would she be able to shoot another person?

CHAPTER 4

*a*fter cleaning the dishes from breakfast, Sadie and Barnaby left the tent and walked away from camp. The spring runoff caused mud during the day and it froze at night. Luckily, the time was still early and the ground remained frozen.

They walked on a well-used path to the forest. Barnaby and her father must have gone this way whenever they left the camp.

Sadie unpacked the weapons from their cases. A Colt 45 pistol and a Winchester lever-action 44-40 carbine. She also had two boxes of ammunition for each gun.

She handed the rifle to Barnaby and put on the holster with the Colt.

He whistled. "I've been wanting one of these for years."

She shrugged. "I don't know anything about guns. I

just wanted something I wouldn't have to reload very often. It's one of the newest rifles available."

He nodded as he caressed the barrel of the rifle as though it was a woman.

Sadie wouldn't mind if he caressed her legs like that. *What am I thinking? He's my partner, not my lover.*

What would he be like as a lover? Would I even know if he's a good or a bad lover since I've never had one?

You could find out. After all, he is your husband.

No. He's my husband in name only. Just for my protection.

Your marriage doesn't have to be in name only.

Yes, it does. Now be quiet.

She stopped talking to herself and concentrated on watching Barnaby.

He turned around and looked at the area they'd stopped. "This'll do."

She followed his gaze and could see the camp and watch for claim jumpers, but they weren't so close she might shoot anything if she got turned around.

He reached into the backpack he was carrying and pulled out five empty cans. "These will work for your targets." He walked about thirty feet in front of them to a downed log and set the cans on top. Then he walked back to her.

Barnaby held out his hand. "May I have your Colt, please?"

She unholstered the weapon and extended it, barrel first.

He side stepped and placed two fingers on the side

of the barrel and pushed it away from him. "Never point a gun at someone unless you mean to shoot them. Pointing it at the ground is the best thing to do."

"Sorry. I wasn't thinking."

"Always stay alert when you're handling a gun. I want you to watch me." He took the gun and checked the load, spinning the cylinder to make sure every slot held a bullet. Then he snapped the cylinder back in place and leveled the gun, pointed at the cans, pulled back the hammer and fired.

One can fell back over the log.

"Now, I want you to do exactly what I did. Can you do that?"

Sadie nodded. "I think so."

He handed her the gun, butt first.

She pointed the gun at the ground, then she opened the chamber and spun it. Then she looked up at Barnaby. "I can't tell where the spent bullet is."

He smiled. "That's right. Unless you look at the front of the open cylinder, you can't really tell. But I don't want you to do that. I'll reload for you." He pulled the hammer back part way and opened the loading gate. Then he took the extractor rod and pressed is against each bullet until the spent one came out. Then he reloaded the gun.

Then she aimed the Colt at the cans and fired. The kick of the gun pushed her arm up in the air and almost knocked her over. She hadn't expected the recoil to be so great even though she was used to the one of the shotgun which was even more.

"Holy cow. Why didn't it do that when you shot it?"

"I have stronger arms than you do, and I was expecting it. You weren't. Now that you know what it will do, use two hands and see if you can keep it level. Try it again."

Taking her time, she gripped the pistol with both hands, aimed and fired. Her arms lifted a little, but they stayed mostly level.

The can, however, didn't move.

She looked up at Barnaby and pouted. "I missed."

He smiled. "Yes, but you definitely scared it."

Sadie looked at him, wide-eyed, and then burst into laughter. "You're hilarious. I like it. If we can laugh every day, we'll be okay."

Chuckling, he pointed toward the gun. "Okay, try it again. From the top."

She followed all the steps he had but still couldn't hit the cans. Frustrated, she stamped a foot. "I'll never get it. Maybe I should just stick to the shotgun."

"Sadie. It will take longer to teach you than just a couple of tries. Now, do it again. You're doing well. You are actually getting close to the cans, and I hadn't expected that at this point. Reload and try again."

She took a deep breath and nodded. Then she expended the spent cartridges and reloaded all the chambers of the cylinder. Holding the pistol with both hands, she aimed and fired. A can fell over. She holstered the gun and then shouted. "I did it! I hit one." She threw her arms around Barnaby's neck and kissed him.

Barnaby put his arms around her waist and smiled. "You certainly did."

Still filled with excitement, Sadie widened her eyes as she instantly remembered where she was. Her pulse raced and her breathing quickened. She unwound her arms from around his neck and moved back. "I'm sorry. I completely lost my head."

He slowly lowered his arms and stepped back. "No harm done."

She couldn't meet his gaze right away, but then looked at him. "Well, shall I try again? I don't want that to be a fluke. I need to make sure I can hit what I aim at with this gun, and then we can move on to the rifle."

Barnaby nodded. "You're right, of course. Let's get some more practice in, then we'll switch weapons."

For the next hour, Sadie practiced with the Colt. She got to where she could pull it from the holster and check the cylinder in one smooth move and then shoot.

"If a man is intent on either having you or the claim, you won't be able to check the cylinder. You need to just shoot, and shoot to kill."

A shiver went up her spine. "I understand. I won't let anyone do me or our claim harm, just as I know you won't. Look at me, Barnaby, really look at me. I'm not some simpering woman here to take advantage of your benevolence. I'm here to work. I'm strong, and I'll take my father's place—just as soon as you teach me to mine gold." She grinned.

He gazed at her, but his eyes remained intense, with

no humor in them. "I intend to teach you all about placer mining."

"What is that? I saw some drawings in a book. It's done with a large, strange-looking pie tin."

Barnaby laughed. "I suppose, if you don't know what it's for, it would look just like that. Maybe I'll have you bake a pie in one, sometime."

"Probably not, since I didn't see an oven, or even a Dutch oven. Do you have either?"

"Actually, we have both. I should have told you, but I'll show you when we get back."

They spent the next two hours shooting the rifle, first Barnaby and then Sadie. Once she remembered to keep the firearm tight against her shoulder, she was fairly consistent and hit most of what she aimed at.

He pointed toward their camp. "Let's head back now. I have some more things to teach you today."

She didn't mind going back. Her arms and legs were aching with all the walking they'd done yesterday and the shooting practice today. She hoped she could rest when they got back.

They packed up the cans and the spent shells.

"Why do you pack up the shells?"

"Because we can reuse them. I have everything to load our shells, and it's cheaper than buying new."

"You're very resourceful."

Sadie walked behind Barnaby on the way back to camp. She wanted to know more about this man she married, but she wasn't sure what she should ask.

When they reached the claim, she started to put the guns in the tent.

"Don't leave them in there except at night or if you are inside during the day. They won't do you any good if you can't reach them quickly."

He led the way to the other side of the tarp with the supplies. There, in the hillside, was a fireplace, for lack of a better description, dug into the permafrost. It was back away from the river and the campsite. She'd been so tired she hadn't noticed many details when they'd arrived yesterday.

Sadie looked at the area, the way they set it up. She smiled and knew her father had done it.

The area was in between two small mounds of dirt. Little hills, she called them. Into one of them a fire pit had been dug. A work table stood across from the fire pit. On the table, or under it, were what could be called fireplace tools...a small garden spade and a broom. Also under the table was a small pile of wood for the fire. A large pile was nearby covered with a tarp to keep it dry and usable.

"Oh, my God. How did you do that? The ground has to be frozen. We don't have the mud around here like in Dawson City."

"We dug it our first summer here. Did you know your father liked to bake? Things other than bread, I mean."

Her eyes widened. "My father? You're kidding, right? I thought he just did the bread and the biscuits out of necessity."

With a sparkle in his eyes, he chuckled. "Not at all. He's the one who baked all our desserts, too, cobblers mostly. I was happy he did so, as my skills leave a lot to be desired."

Sadie shrugged. "Well, I love to bake, too, so I guess I'll be doing our baking."

He nodded. "Yes, unless you want either raw or burned biscuits. Given my skills or lack thereof."

"That's fine. I'm not so good with regular cooking except for breakfast. As long as you have lunch and dinner, I'll bake and do breakfast."

They walked back to the tent, and since she intended to rest inside, she grabbed the guns.

Barnaby went inside, sat on his cot, and then stretched out.

She leaned the rifle against the tent near the opening and set the holster at the foot of her cot. Then she lay on her side to face him. Finally, she got up the nerve to ask what was on her mind. "Barnaby, how old are you?"

"I'm thirty-four and you?"

"Twenty-seven. Why haven't you married before now?"

He shrugged. "Who's to say I haven't?"

She popped up an eyebrow. "Well, were you?"

He didn't look at her. "Yes."

She waited for him to continue. *Dragging an answer out of him is like getting a tooth pulled.* "What happened?"

"She died," he whispered.

"I'm sorry. How did she die?"

55

Barnaby studied her. "You're a nosy one, aren't you?"

She lifted her chin a bit. "I am and I'm sorry for being insensitive, but I should know about the man I married, just as you should know about me."

"Fine, you go first."

"Very well. When I was twenty, I was engaged to a wonderful man. His name was Richard, and I loved him very much. But his family didn't approve of me. I wasn't rich enough. When he broke it off, it devastated me. Father said he wanted me to have what he and Mother did. They were in love right until the day she died. But..." she looked down. Her hands were shaking, and she clasped them, hoping he didn't see. "I'm cursed. Everyone I love leaves me. First my mother, then my grandmother, followed by Richard, and now my father. How many more people do I have to lose?" She turned around, her eyes full of tears.

Barnaby stood and sat beside her, placing an arm around her shoulders.

She kept her head down. "Sadie, look at me."

Lifting her chin, her eyes filled with tears, she gazed at him.

"People die. We often don't know why. Influenza took my wife and son while I chased my dream of finding gold in California. I never should have taken them with me, but Bessie refused to be parted. My son was only two months old when we began the trip."

How horrible. Such a sad situation. "How long ago did they die?"

"Three years. But you never forget your first love or your child. He was just a baby, seven months old. I'm just glad he was too young to know what was happening. Unlike Bessie, who knew everything. She knew she was dying and so was Bobby. That fact bothered her more than anything, that her sweet baby was dying, too."

Sadie couldn't help the tears that filled her eyes at his story. He, too, had lost so much and now she'd taken away from him having an actual marriage and children. She realized she had cursed herself, again, to also never having children. But they would have to have a genuine marriage and relations before she could even think about having children. Could she do that?

Someday, she would gather the courage to face him and understand it was the right time. But what if she never did? What if the right time never presented itself? Was she wrong for waiting for something to happen? Waiting for some sign to tell her Barnaby was the one? And if he isn't the one, did it actually matter? He was her husband until death did them part.

He stood and secured the tent flap. Then he stopped tying it and cocked his head. "What are you thinking so hard about?"

She was honest. "I was thinking about children and how you get them."

He straightened his neck and raised a challenging eyebrow. "You know what must happen before you can have children, don't you?"

Sadie rolled her eyes and put her hands on her hips. "I'm twenty-seven years old. I'm not stupid."

Barnaby advanced on her, wrapped an arm around her waist, and pulled her close. "You might not be stupid, but you are very naïve." He lowered his mouth to hers and kissed her hard, then he gentled and pulled back. "If I were not a gentleman, I could take you anytime I wanted, and you could do little about it. Think about that, Sadie, and then tell me you can take care of yourself." He turned away.

Tears filled her eyes. He was right, and she knew it. But she'd felt nothing like she had when he kissed her. He meant the kiss to punish her, but she'd started to wrap her arms around his neck at the moment he let her go. Her heart had pounded, first out of fear, then with something else. She liked the kiss and wanted more. She stood still in somewhat of a stupor, remembering his lips on hers. Reaching up, she touched them, knowing they were swollen.

Barnaby turned his gaze toward her. His mouth ticked up on one side in a smile. He was aware of the impact he had on her and, based on his smile...he took pleasure in it.

"Darn him," she said under her breath. Her hands fisted, and she wished she had his neck in her hands. She'd squeeze that smirk off his face. Instead, she sat on her cot and brooded. She didn't have much else to do. She wouldn't go for a walk, she'd most likely get lost, so she sat.

As agreed that night, Barnaby prepared their

dinner. She'd brought tinned beef and purchased real potatoes in Dawson City, while he bought sourdough bread.

The meal, though not fancy, was good and filled her stomach.

Barnaby ate his serving and everything that was left.

The man was big and had an enormous appetite, which Sadie didn't begrudge him. She liked the fact that he was large enough he could protect her against most foes.

"What will you teach me tomorrow? When will we dig for gold?"

He shook his head and tore off another chunk of bread. "We pan for gold, remember? You'll be learning that tomorrow."

She and Barnaby sat on their cots facing one another. "I don't know why I'm so tired." She yawned.

Both she and Barnaby were thankful for the extra blankets she'd brought. And she put on a stocking cap like Barnaby told her to. She stayed warm between her father's covers and hers. His cologne still scented them, albeit faintly.

The next morning, she awoke early and made their coffee. Ice crystals covered the roof of the tent, which didn't surprise her. The night was so cold she'd slept in her clothes. Before she went out to relieve herself and returned to make the coffee, she'd donned her coat and the pistol, knowing she couldn't be too careful. She left her gloves in her pocket so she could use her hands and wished she could wear them. It didn't take any time at all for her fingers to feel frozen...and this was the spring. What would the weather be like in winter? She wasn't sure she was eager to know.

Barnaby was up when she returned.

He grumbled, "Good morning." Then he left the tent.

Their camp stove had its own metal stove pipe to conduct the smoke out of the tent. They made the stove from half a metal barrel with a door for loading wood into the barrel. Over that was the cooking surface, which was big enough to hold two skillets or one skillet and the coffeepot. Halfway up the stovepipe was a warming oven.

Once the coffee had boiled, she removed it and cooked the eggs and bacon like yesterday, except today she added slices of skillet-toasted bread. She put a little bacon grease on one side of the bread and fried it in the hot skillet until it was a golden brown.

Barnaby returned while she was dishing up the plates.

She added the first two toasted slices to Barnaby's plate and toasted two more. She dished up the eggs and bacon just like yesterday before putting a third slice of bread on Barnaby's plate.

"So, you are teaching me to pan for gold today, right?"

Barnaby nodded because his mouth was full. After he swallowed, he lifted a hand and pointed toward the river. "Most of the claims are farther up the river.

That's why we have so much land around us. They left plenty of gold for us to gather because a lot of the miners are only interested in getting the gold they can pick up with their hands. They aren't willing to work for it. That's part of the reason there are so many claim jumpers."

She scoffed. "I have no use for lazy men."

"I could have been lazy and you wouldn't have known it."

"Wrong. My father wouldn't have partnered with that type of man."

Barnaby laughed. "You're right. John wouldn't have. He was a hard worker and expected the same from his partner. As I do."

"I'm sure if you give me some time to get acclimated to," she waved her arms over her head. "everything, that I'll be fine and you'll be happy to have me here."

After cleaning up the tent and doing the dishes, she and Barnaby were ready to head out to the river.

She dressed in her rubber boots, two pairs of long johns and her wool pants, which she tucked inside the boots. She also wore a wool shirt in case she got too warm with her coat on, plus she thought it might be easier to work without the coat.

Barnaby took her to the river's edge. "I'll show you how it's done and then let you try it." He kneeled and used a flat, wide pan to scoop up some gravel and water. Then he swirled the mixture around, letting it run out over the rim of the pan into the river again. He did this until very little of the gravel was left. Then he reached down and picked up a gold nugget and held it up. "Most people would have missed this because it's so small. But I don't care if it's just one flake, I pick it up and put it in my bag." He opened the top of a drawstring leather bag hanging from his belt and put the little nugget inside. "Now I want you to try it."

Sadie squatted and did everything he'd done. The first time she'd dipped the pan into the river she had to clench her teeth lest she cry out at the freezing water. That time she found nothing. Same for the second and third and fourth time. "I must not be doing something right. I'm not finding anything." She stood, set the pan on the bank, shook her hands dry and then pressed her hands into her back to relieve the ache. "I can't believe you do that all day long. How do you manage?"

He waved off the question. "You get used to it, but it's hard, back-breaking work. Don't ever think it's not."

"I can see that, with the little I've done. But I'll manage, and I won't let either of us down." She dropped to her knees, like he was, and started working the river again.

An hour or so later, her back was killing her. She vowed to take a break after this last pan. She was down to mostly water when something glittered in the bottom. She reached down and plucked a nugget the size of her thumbnail out of the sediment. Then she screamed. "Barnaby! Look. Look what I found." Sadie got to her feet and met him as he was on his way to her. "Is it good?"

He put out his hand.

She dropped the nugget into it.

Barnaby turned it over in his palm and then grinned before tucking it into his leather bag. Then he wrapped his arms around her waist and swung her in a circle before setting her down again.

"You did very good. That's worth more than I've found all last week." He looked down and caught her gaze. "This makes all the hard work worth the effort. Didn't I tell you there was gold here?"

Sadie quickly regained her balance when he set her down. Now, if her heart would stop pounding and she didn't feel like her insides were turning over. "You did, and now I can see that for myself. What is it you hope to get, Barnaby? Just to be rich? Or to do something? I want to be independent, so I don't rely on any man for my survival."

"I've always wanted to own a ranch, free and clear. I don't want to owe anyone anything."

She was glad to discover he had a goal. It was one she could get behind. If he wanted a ranch, she supposed she would go, too.

Was this what attraction felt like? Was she attracted to Barnaby Drake? Was that why she thought about going with him...no, wanted to go with him?

CHAPTER 5

*A*fter a long day of panning for gold, Sadie was thrilled she didn't have to cook. All she wanted to do was lie on the cot and sleep for days. Her back hurt. Her legs and knees hurt, plus her legs from the knees down were wet, despite her rubber boots.

Before she sat on her cot and stretched out, she took off her boots, socks, and pants. Her long johns were damp but not wet.

"You need to take off your long johns, too, " he said as he set up the stove to cook supper. "Anything that's wet needs to come off. It will freeze overnight, and you'll never get warm. The heat from the stove tonight and again in the morning will help dry them. I hope you brought another pair so you can switch them out. You'll be a lot more comfortable in dry clothes. Keeping them clean is another matter, altogether."

"I did." She chewed her bottom lip, wondering if she

should ask him to turn around or just get the job done. She must have waited too long.

He finally shook his head.

"I'll be outside. Let me know when you're done changing."

"I will...thank you."

As he opened the tent's flaps and stepped out, he snorted.

Sadie hurried and changed into the dry long johns. She'd pulled on dry pants next. "I'm decent now. You can come back inside."

Barnaby pulled back the tent flap. He tied it closed and settled on his cot. "Doesn't it feel better to be dry?"

"Yes, definitely. What about you? You need to put on dry clothes." She grabbed the coffeepot and then lit the stove. When the kindling lit the wood and the fire was going well, she shut the door and placed the pot on the top.

"I do, but I'm not about to make you stand outside in the cold to protect your delicate sensibilities. I suggest that we simply turn our backs or even read something so we don't make you uncomfortable."

She stood by the stove, her hands on her hips. "And I suppose you're not embarrassed?"

"I'm a man. That sort of thing doesn't bother me."

She pressed her lips together. "Hmpft. Figures. Well, don't worry about my delicate sensibilities. We're partners and that means, in this case, that we live and work in close quarters. I'll become used to it." *How in the world will I get used to it? I never even saw father's bare chest. I can't imagine seeing Barnaby's.*

"Fine. I'll prepare supper, per our agreement. When will you be baking bread?"

"Now that I'm dry, I'll make a batch of biscuits, if you like. I'll need to light the fire outside. Then tomorrow, I'll start a couple loaves of sourdough to rise while we are working. I'll have to quit earlier than usual to get them into the oven you and Daddy dug above the fireplace outside. I'll need the starter and a recipe. Did he have one?"

"I think so. In his footlocker."

"All right I'll look."

He shrugged. "It's easy. Every week, I add about one-third of a cup of water and a tablespoon or two of flour and mix it all together, usually by shaking the jar."

"And that feeds the starter?"

"Yes. I don't know the whys and wherefores. It just does." He put his hands on his pillow behind his head and stared at the ceiling.

"So, what's for supper?"

He sat up on the cot and swung his legs over the side. "You brought canned meat and milk. I figure to make a gravy to go over those biscuits you're about to make." He grinned.

"All right, I get the idea. I'm on my way." She stood and pulled on a clean wool shirt and rolled up the sleeves, leaving her long johns to protect her arms from the cold. She'd given up trying to wear a corset with her mining clothes. It was too difficult. Then she went outside, started a fire in the fireplace and retrieved the Dutch oven.

By the time she'd settled the Dutch oven in the fire with hot coals on the lid, she could smell the meat cooking. She imagined that several of the cans of meat would go into the gravy in order for it to be enough food for Barnaby. Goodness, that man was big.

She imagined how surprised Cook would be that she was applying what the woman had taught her. If it hadn't been for her, Sadie wouldn't know anything about cooking.

Now that she knew about the altitude, she thought it would take about fifteen minutes for the biscuits to bake and went to tell Barnaby.

She opened the tent, and the wonderful aroma flooded her senses. "My goodness, why is it food smells so much better out here in the wilderness?"

He sat by the stove and stirred the gravy. "You're hungrier, I expect."

She sat on her cot to wait for the biscuits. "I am that. I haven't been this hungry in ages. Of course, I've never worked so hard in my life. Is every day like this? Do you ever take a day off?"

"It is, and I do. When I go to town is a day off. I try to make it down and back in one day. I don't like to leave the claim for long because of the claim jumpers."

She crossed her legs and leaned back with her arms supporting her from behind. "Well, now that I'm here, we don't have to worry about claim jumpers. You go to town, and I'll stay and work the claim." She grinned. "Or maybe I'll lie about all day eating bon-bons."

"I'm not leaving you here alone. You could get hurt or worse once the claim jumpers learn you're a woman. That won't happen."

"I know how to shoot the pistol now, and I'll wear it all the time. If I have it and the shotgun, I'll be fine. You'll leave in the morning and return in the evening as usual. I'm not spending the night up here alone, but you won't have Homer trying to take our property for his own." She stood, went to him and patted his head. "Trust me. I'll be okay."

Barnaby shook his head, knocking away her hand. "That won't be happening. I won't need to go to town for a couple of months now that you brought all these supplies and maybe not even then. I only went for potatoes and a few other supplies. Eggs, if I can find them. One time, I saw some man with chickens for sale. They were gone before I could even get close." He stirred the gravy. "Are your biscuits ready?"

She stood. "They should be shortly." She pulled a pocket watch out and checked the time. "They've got five more minutes."

"I'll take the gravy off the stove until you return with the biscuits, so it doesn't overcook." He removed the skillet and moved it over to the table.

"Thanks. I'll check them and see if they are ready. I'm only guessing the time to bake them up here." She left the tent and walked back out to the baking area.

Sadie brushed the coals from the lid of the Dutch

oven back into the fire. Wearing her leather gloves, she picked up the pot and set it on the table, where she removed the lid. While the biscuits cooled a bit she walked back to the tent and got a plate.

When she returned with the plate piled high with fresh hot biscuits, she saw Barnaby had dished up the gravy into their pie tins.

They sat at the table with the quick bread between them and ate.

Sadie didn't think she'd ever been so hungry. The gravy was delicious, it was smooth and savory, and she ate her fill.

Silence reigned while they ate with both of them too hungry to talk.

Barnaby cleaned the gravy up using several more biscuits and probably could have eaten more than that.

"I really need to bake a cobbler or something for after dinner."

He licked his lips. "I'd be mighty grateful if you did. I don't normally get sweets except if I go to town and then it costs so much, I usually don't. But I noticed you brought cans of fruit."

"Actually, I've got the time right now. They're really easy to do and I left the fire burning. Plus the Dutch oven is empty." She stood and started to leave but turned back. "We should think about getting a second Dutch oven, then I could bake the biscuits and the cobbler at the same time."

He nodded. "Good idea. Next time we're in town, we'll go to the hardware store."

"Great." She left through the tent flap.

Later, after dessert was ready and Sadie chuckled to herself as she watched Barnaby eat all the cobbler except her bowlful. They played cards for about an hour before her exhaustion made her crawl into her cot.

She slept in her long johns and hung her clothes over the foot of her bed. Too tired to even think about whether Barnaby was looking, she'd simply taken off her clothes and got under the blankets.

Sadie lay there for a while, but sleep wouldn't come. Light still shone in the tent. If he turned over toward her, she'd see his face and could read his expressions. "Barnaby?" She flipped to her side and watched his silhouette, then whispered, so that if he was asleep, she wouldn't wake him.

"Yes?"

"Does the mercantile have mattresses for these cots?"

"They do."

"Why didn't you and Father get any?"

"We didn't think it was necessary, and they were expensive."

"I think we'd be warmer if we had them. We should pick some up next time we're in town."

He turned toward her, frowning. "We still don't have the money."

"I still have some money. I didn't spend it all getting here, though that cost a pretty nickel. And we have Lucky to carry them back."

The corner of his mouth crooked up like he was chewing the inside of his cheek while in thought.

"Okay. The mattresses would make sleeping more comfortable for both of us."

She grinned. "Great. I can't wait until we get them." She crossed her arms behind her head. The tent was still warm from the stove, so she wasn't cold, but she knew by morning it would be freezing again.

The last two days with Barnaby had been the toughest and most exhilarating of her life. She truly felt alive, not just existing.

She thought Barnaby was a strange man...at once gruff and still a gentleman. She found that combination very attractive, which was good, since he was her husband.

He could have taken her on their wedding night or any time since they'd been on the claim. But he hadn't. She liked him a lot. Would she be better off keeping him as a friend? Or actually making him her husband?

HOMER WATCHED the camp from the shadow of the trees. It looked like Barnaby's new partner was a woman. He heard in town he'd gotten married, but he didn't put any faith in such gossip. Too few women for things like that to be true. Yet, here he was, watching her pan for gold and then cooking something in that fancy fireplace Barnaby and John had dug out of the hillside.

A woman.

He could do many things with a woman besides making her cook for him. She'd see to his every need, or he'd make sure she'd wish she had. All he had to do was wait for Barnaby to be gone to town or hunting for the day. Then Homer could have his way with Barnaby's woman and when he returned, Homer would kill him and take his woman and his claim.

Chuckling quietly to himself, he walked back to his claim through knee-high snow in the forest and over the frozen ground nearer the river. He'd spent every nickel he had to get the provisions the Canadians required before they'd let anyone in to their country and to the gold fields. So he, at least, had the some of the necessities...shelter and water. He was likely out of most everything else, because he couldn't cook or hunt properly, and he had spent the small amount of gold he'd found on whiskey and women.

If he had that woman, he wouldn't need but the whiskey. No man in his right mind would give up that, even for a woman. And since he knew she could pan for gold, she could do the work while he stayed warm and dry. Now that he saw her, he knew if he had that woman, his existence would be greatly improved.

* * *

FOR THE NEXT SIX WEEKS, Sadie and Barnaby worked side-by-side, ate together and slept in the same tent.

Yet, he made no advances to show he had any interest in making their marriage a real one.

Maybe she should test the waters and ask him directly. Her father would turn over in his grave if he had one, if he knew what she was doing. Not only the working of the claim, but being married to his partner. Or would he? He'd obviously liked Barnaby enough to file for a gold claim with him. Why wouldn't he be happy she'd married his friend?

That night, over supper, she told him her thoughts. "Barnaby, I want to go to town for those mattresses, and I'd like to stay overnight."

He frowned and narrowed his eyes. "You know I hate to be away from the claim that long. Homer will try to take over again and I just might have to kill him this time. What do you want besides the mattresses?" He sipped on his coffee and leaned back in his chair.

She clasped her hands and circled her thumbs around each other before looking up. "I want us to stay overnight." She lifted a hand. "Wait until you hear me out. You're my husband, for better or for worse, until one of us departs this earth. I want to have children someday, and...and...oh, dang it, this is harder than I thought."

"Just say it, Sadie. I don't want to misunderstand you, and I need to hear you say what you want."

She took a deep breath and let it out. Then she took another. "Oh, all right. I don't want to lose my virginity on a mattress in a tent. I want a proper bed when we consummate this marriage. There, I said it." She dropped her gaze to her hands again.

Barnaby was silent.

The next thing she knew, he was beside her with a knuckle on her chin, turning it toward him.

"Look at me, Sadie."

She slowly lifted her lids and gazed into his dark, smoldering blue eyes.

"I don't want to misunderstand. You are a virgin?"

She nodded. Her stomach still roiled, and her hands shook.

"Are you sure this is what you want?" His voice was quiet, gentle.

She nodded again. "I'm sure. I've been thinking about it a lot. I want to have children and we must be husband and wife in deed, as well as in name, for that to happen."

He smiled and his eyes twinkled. "Yes, we do. But you want to wait until we go to town, right?"

She straightened, determined not to make love here. "I do. I want to be in a bed, a proper bed, for my first time. Is that wrong? To want to be comfortable?"

He ran a finger down her cheek. "There is nothing wrong with that *mo ghra*. Not a thing. And I believe you're right, you deserve it. We'll head to town tomorrow."

Suddenly, her stomach turned over and over so much she thought she would lose her supper. "There's no hurry. I just wanted to let you know my plans."

"*Mo ghra*, I've been waiting for you to decide you

wanted an actual marriage. What we have on paper was necessary to get you here, but I don't believe in divorce, and I would guess you don't either. Though the thought of children puts me off, but we'll figure it out if it happens."

She looked at him askance. "Don't you want children?"

A shadow fell over his face. "Children have no place in the life we lead. It's too dangerous and there's too much sickness. They could die."

"It's possible, I suppose, but you and I could die, too. Look at my father. Buried in an avalanche that turned into his grave. You don't even know where in that mountain of snow he is, do you? You only have to know his circumstances to know he died too young."

Sadness stirred behind his eyes, and he gazed at the floor. "I don't, only saw him go down. He was a grown man. He had choices. My son never had a choice or a chance."

Sadie saw how unhappy Barnaby was and wasn't sure she could have a child with him. But he was her husband. Could she resign herself to never having children?

CHAPTER 6

Sadie was lost in thought the entire trip to Dawson City. Barnaby seemed as well since the entire trip was quiet, with only the sounds of birds chirping or taking flight and the clomp of the horse's hooves breaking the silence.

They both rode Lucky with Sadie sitting mostly on Barnaby's lap the entire way. Riding Lucky cut the time to town in half. When they arrived, it was lunchtime. They walked into the hotel.

Kitty stood behind the desk.

Barnaby took off his hat. "Hi, Kitty."

"Hello, Kitty," said Sadie.

She looked up from her paperwork. "Well, if it isn't the Drakes as I live and breathe. I haven't seen you two for a couple of months. How is married life treating you?"

"We're fine. We're about to go next door and get a bite to eat. We'd like to have baths when we get back, and can you keep this until we finish eating?" He set a carpetbag on the desk.

She smiled. "Sure, and I'll start the water heating now."

"We'd like two tubs, please," said Sadie.

"Sure. I'll get those up there now." She stopped. "On second thought, I'll put you in Room 110. It's at the back and should be quieter than the front rooms. And it will save my men from carrying those buckets up the stairs. Seems no matter how careful they try to be, I end up with wet carpet."

"That'll be fine," said Barnaby.

She handed him the key.

"We'll be back later." Barnaby placed a hand on Sadie's waist and guided her to the restaurant.

Sadie lifted her nose and sniffed. Wonderful scents surrounded her and made her mouth water. Whatever they were cooking smelled heavenly. Of course, whatever they were preparing was more palatable than they'd had in a while, though Barnaby tried and so did Sadie. But for her part, there were only so many ways to prepare oatmeal or make cornmeal mush. After they were seated, she looked up at the chalkboard with the day's specials and then back at Barnaby. "What are elk medallions? I've never heard of that cut of meat."

"They are just slices of the back strap which runs up and down both sides of the spine. It's shaped like a long skinny loaf of bread so that when it's sliced, it makes a circular piece of meat, like a medallion. It's a very tender cut of meat. You'll like them."

"Okay. I'll have those."

When the waitress came, Sadie gave her the order. She had to speak loudly because of the sounds of talking and laughter from the men in the surrounding room. As usual, except for her and the two waitresses, everyone was a man.

The waitress couldn't have been over five feet tall. She had black hair and dark brown eyes and was very curvy. "I'll have the medallions and whatever the daily stew is."

She put her pad back in her apron pocket. "What can I get you all to drink?"

Sadie kept her hands in her lap. "I'll have coffee, please. With milk and sugar."

"You're lucky. We just got our supplies in, so we have condensed milk." She turned toward Barnaby. "And for you, Barnaby?"

"Coffee, black."

"Gotcha," said the waitress.

"Thanks, Sally."

"You betcha." She turned and headed toward the kitchen.

Sadie lifted a brow. "Do you know all the women in town by name?"

His cheeks colored, the color rising to his forehead. "Not all."

She laughed. "Don't worry. I'm not jealous, just curious."

"I'm not worried about whether you're jealous or not. I'm a man, and there aren't a lot of women here, in case you hadn't noticed, and the ones that are you pay by the hour, or less sometimes. Depends on the girl."

Sadie sat with her back straight, and her wrists crossed on the table. "I'm sorry. I shouldn't judge. I don't know what I'd do if I had to make a living that way. I don't think I could."

He lowered his voice. "You're a virgin still and probably still a wealthy woman, which is why I still don't understand why you're here. But regardless of your moral code, desperate people do desperate things."

She shook her head and sighed. Then she pulled her hands back to her lap and "I'm not wealthy any more. I spent a lot of what I had on the trip here and to prepare for living here. Admittedly, I didn't scrimp on either expenditure. I sold everything so I could come here. My father's friend, who was also his man of business, said I could probably live comfortably on it for a year. More if I was frugal, I might make it longer. But I wouldn't have my house. I'd have to move to a small apartment. And then I'd have to find a job I'd probably hate just so I could continue to survive." She stared hard at Barnaby. "I feel more alive than I ever have before. I'm doing something for me and not just to survive. Who knows what we'll find next? We've found some decent-sized nuggets in the last two months, and I think we'll find more. I'm paying for our time here in town and the mattresses and whatever else we need until my money runs out, which will be soon at the prices in Dawson City. I want to keep the money from the gold for a rainy day." Looking for any change in his expression, she continued to stare. "So, what do you think?"

* * *

WHAT DID HE THINK? Barnaby smiled at his wife. He would say little wife, but there was nothing little about Sadie Thompson—no, Sadie Drake. She was all woman and probably the strongest woman he'd ever known. The fact she was his wife and now wanted that to be a reality pleased him, but the thought of having children paralyzed him from the inside out.

"I think that's an excellent idea. I'd like to keep the money separate, as well, even though now that we're married, everything you have belongs to me."

She leaned forward, and her eyes narrowed. "You? You!"

He lifted his hand as she sputtered her outrage. "Calm down and lower your voice. I don't have any notion of keeping anything of yours, and we'll split the gold in half as we agreed."

She blinked several times, sat back, and took a couple of deep breaths. "No one can hear us, there's too much noise. I'm sorry. I know that's the law, however much I abhor it. Thank you for not taking all my money. Besides, I'm only using it to make our life a little easier."

"That you are. And I appreciate it. So we're agreed. You will spend your cash, and we'll save the gold."

"Yes. Thank you."

Sally returned with the coffee and their meals on a tray.

Seeing how much Sadie enjoyed adding the sugar and milk to her coffee amused him. Both were rare commodities in Dawson City. He wondered how Kitty kept them in stock. The way into the town was getting easier, at least in the spring and summer. Coming over either Chilkoot or White Mountain Pass was difficult for most of the year, but the trek was easier in the warmer months and now there was the tram.

Regardless of which way the gold seekers used, they still had to traverse the Yukon River and hundreds of miles of rapids to reach Dawson City. This alone made it amazing that Dawson City had the variety of goods available that it did.

Barnaby shuddered, remembering his and John's harrowing trip down the river. John had almost drowned. Barnaby had tied him to the boat to keep him from falling out.

He shook his head to let go of the memory and sipped his coffee.

"You seemed way off yonder somewhere." Sadie cut a piece from a medallion and put it in her mouth.

"I was just remembering something. Nothing important." *Now. It had been pretty important then.*

Her eyes flashed open wide. "Wow, this is delicious. It's so tender and is juicy. There is a freshness to it I've never had with beef."

He smiled. "Elk, if it's butchered right, is very lean

meat that has a slight gamey flavor to it, but I think that's mostly from what the animal eats. They don't get any hay or grain. Sometimes, it's too strong, and the meat is only good for stews or chili."

"Well, this doesn't seem to be too strong. It's wonderful." She cut another piece off and then made noises of appreciation.

Barnaby had a hard time waiting for her to finish her meal. He'd already finished his and was eager to go to the room and get a bath and then make love to his virgin little wife. He would make sure she enjoyed it. If he didn't, she wouldn't want to do it again, and he absolutely wouldn't want that.

He'd been attracted to Sadie since he first saw her causing a ruckus at the saloon. And then when she'd fallen face first, after he laughed, all he wanted to do was lift her up and tell her all would be well. He'd eventually carried her, and she'd felt so right in his arms, he hadn't wanted to let go. And now she was his wife, to have and to hold, and he expected to hold her and make passionate love to her...if she hadn't changed her mind.

Finally, she finished and dabbed her mouth with her napkin.

"I'm ready. I hope they have plenty of hot water. I'm soaking until my muscles are limp."

He chuckled. "I don't think they have enough hot water in the town for the time you would like to soak."

"You're probably right." She stood.

Barnaby stood too, put a hand on her back at her

waist and guided her out of the restaurant and to the hotel's front desk.

Kitty was still there.

"We're ready for those baths now."

She smiled. "I'll send the men over right away." She turned and walked through a curtain to their left.

"Let's go to the room and wait." He guided her again down the hall to the right of the desk.

Theirs was the last room on the right. Kitty had been correct; the sounds of the street were much quieter.

"Oh, my." Sadie raised a hand to her mouth. "This is a much bigger room than the one I had before." She turned toward Barnaby. "And look. She brought us towels." She pointed at the bed where several towels sat. On top were two washcloths with two bars of soap. "It was so kind of Kitty to provide us with soap, too. Do you suppose she gave us the honeymoon suite?"

The room was half again bigger than Sadie's first room. The bed was the same size but with white iron head and foot boards. The nightstands, bureau with attached mirror and chest of drawers were all painted white. The wallpaper was cream colored with red roses attached to green vines streaming through it.

Each side of the bed had plenty of room for a bathtub.

Sadie set the carpetbag with their clean clothes in it on the bureau. She bent over and unlaced her boots and removed them.

"If she has one, this could be it. I'm not aware of every room or what they look like."

She smiled up at him. "No, of course, you aren't. I didn't mean you'd seen them all, just that in your talks with her, she might have mentioned it."

"We didn't have any personal talks. Kitty is a businesswoman, and I was a patron of her businesses. That's all."

A knock sounded at the door.

* * *

THE SOUND STARTLED SADIE, probably because she'd been living in a tent for months where no one knocked. She was pleased her bath was now only minutes away. Her body was aching in anticipation of the hot water.

Barnaby answered the knock and opened the door wide.

"We're here with the tubs you requested, sir."

"Yes, please set one on this side of the bed and one on the other side. Thank you." Barnaby pointed to the spots he meant.

The men did his bidding. The first two each carried a large metal tub. The third man carried buckets of hot water, which he emptied into the tub on the far side of the bed.

"We'll be right back with more hot water." The tallest of the men, who had carried one tub, tipped his hat toward Sadie. "Ma'am."

Sadie, who held her hands clasped in front of her, nodded back. "Sir, could you also bring a pan I can use to rinse my hair?"

"Certainly, ma'am."

The men returned three more times with buckets. The first time, the tall man brought a pan in one bucket. He set down the buckets and handed her the pan after he dried the bottom with a towel he had on his shoulder. "Here you go, ma'am."

Sadie took the pan. "Thank you." She carried it to the far side of the bed. "And could you leave one bucket full so I can rinse the soap from my hair?"

"Certainly. I'll bring you a bucket full of hot water just for that," said the man.

The tubs were half full and perfect for soaking.

Returning quickly with her water, the man set it down.

Barnaby gave him a tip.

"Thank you, sir."

Barnaby locked the door behind him.

She looked over at him. "I guess we'd better undress before this water gets cold."

"Would you like me to turn my back?"

She shook her head. "We're about to see each other naked, anyway. At least that's the way I understand it."

"You are correct, but I...we...won't do anything you don't like. I promise. If something makes you uncomfortable, just tell me, and I'll stop."

"What if you can't stop? I've heard some acquaintances talking about how he couldn't stop no matter how hard she tried. She said it was awful." Her heart pounded and her breathing became erratic as fear gripped her.

Barnaby came to her and took her in his arms. "The person who did that wasn't a man, he was a villain...an animal. They should have arrested him for assault. A real man will stop and won't hurt you. I promise, I'm a real man. Do you trust me?"

She cocked her head and gazed up at him, noticing the firm line of his mouth and the sincerity in his gaze. Did she trust him? "Yes, I do. I don't believe you'd hurt me on purpose."

He nodded. "I won't, though I will tell you there will be a little pain the first time we make love because you are a virgin."

"I understand. Although we'll see each other naked during love-making, I've changed my mind. Could you please face away while I undress for the tub?"

"Of course. You are a little shy, and that is under-standable." He turned around.

She swiftly discarded her dirty clothes and stepped into the hot water and sat. The experience was aston-ishing, as if she had never experienced a hot bath before. Her body instantly relaxed. "You can turn around now." Her head was just above the bed and she watched as he undressed...unable to look away.

Barnaby turned and pulled his sweater over his head. Then he stepped out of his pants, having already discarded his boots. Finally, he took off his long johns and stepped into the water. He leaned back. "This is the life. I don't believe I've ever enjoyed a bath more."

"It is wonderful. I can feel my muscles relaxing as we speak." She'd placed her washcloth over the rim of the metal tub before she leaned her back against it. Then she slid down until only her head and knees were out of the water. "I definitely could get used to this."

"So could I. But our little stove can't handle much more than a pan of water to wash our face and hands."

"We can use the fire for the oven, but the first buckets would get cold before we heat the last ones. Hmm. I guess it's just not practical."

For the next fifteen minutes, they were silent...both of them taking advantage of the hot water.

Sadie soaked until her fingers wrinkled. Then she sat up and washed her body followed by her hair. Rinsing it would be a problem. She reclined in the tub, rinsing out as much soap as she could, and then used the pan and the water in the extra bucket to complete the process.

She wrapped her head with a towel and squeezed as much water out as possible. Then she wrapped a towel around her body.

She stepped out of the tub, turned her back to Barnaby, and dried her body.

When she was done, she dropped the wet towels to the floor near the bathtub. Then she pulled out a clean shirt and put it on before setting the carpetbag on the floor.

Barnaby turned around and gazed at her. "Why are you getting dressed?"

"Because I don't want to be naked or in bed when they come to get the tubs. Aren't you going to tell them to come get them?"

"I am." He smiled. "Later. Much later. For now, I'd like to explore what is under that shirt."

Her face heated as she unbuttoned the shirt. "What do you want me to do? Take it off?"

"Let me." He leisurely slid one sleeve down her shoulder and then the other.

The sleeves stopped at her elbow.

He pushed them down off her arms and let the shirt slide to the floor in a puddle around her feet.

"You are totally mine now." He wrapped his arms around her waist and brought her closer. Then he lowered his head and his lips met hers.

His kiss was gentle, and then he pressed his tongue against the seam of her lips.

"Oh," she said, her eyes wide.

He entered her mouth with his tongue. Then he was exploring her. Tasting her and urging her to taste him.

She touched her tongue to his, liking his taste of coffee and the gravy from the stew he'd eaten.

He pulled back. "You're amazing, Sadie. I can't believe you're mine."

She furrowed her brows. "Who else's would I be?"

He chuckled. Then he bent, picked her up into his arms and deposited her in the middle of the bed. "We're going to take this slow. I want to get to know you and your body. I want to learn the things you like...and for you to get used to my body."

She ran her hands along his arms, feeling the muscles quiver at her touch. "You're so much bigger than I am."

"Don't worry about that, *mo ghra*, we were made for each other. Trust me, okay?"

Sadie nodded. "I trust you, Barnaby."

He came up on one elbow beside her. Then he ran his fingers lightly down her arms, over her chest and her stomach, carefully avoiding her breasts.

Her stomach fluttered, and the center of her femininity throbbed. "Barnaby, what are you doing to me?"

"I'm learning what you like. How do you feel, Sadie?"

"Like my world will explode if you stop."

"Then I won't stop." He kissed her deeply.

All her feelings came to a head. She'd never felt so wonderful. His touch was tender and gentle. He didn't seem in a hurry to get the deed over with. Barnaby was taking his time with her.

He finally touched her breasts.

She melted before him.

Later, much later, he made love to her. Slow, passionate love.

She fell in love with her husband that night. What would she do now if he didn't love her back?

CHAPTER 7

*S*unshine shone through the curtains. Sadie lay with her back curled into Barnaby's stomach, his right arm around her waist. She barely needed a blanket with him holding her like that.

"You're awake." His gravelly voice sounded in her ear.

"I am. And I can see you are, too. I need to get up, though, and I can't with you holding me."

"I like holding you." His voice was gravelly against her ear.

His dark arm stood out against the white of her stomach. "I like it, too, under most circumstances, but I must get up."

He lifted his arm.

She rolled away and did her morning business behind a screen before returning to his warm embrace.

"Now, you've done it. You've awakened the beast. I'll be right back."

When he returned to bed, he pulled her close. He moved her hair out of the way and kissed her neck just below her ear.

She shivered as a wave of pleasure traveled through her.

"Barnaby. Why did we only make love once last night? I know you wanted more. I could tell." As heat traveled up her neck to her face, she wished she didn't blush so readily.

"*Mo ghra*, it was your first time, and whether you knew it, you were sore from our lovemaking. Today, you'll be better, and there won't be any more pain when we make love."

She rolled to her back and opened her eyes wide. "Really? Are you sure? Because I would like to make love again."

He rose up on one elbow. "Never let it be said that Barnaby Drake left a woman wanting."

Leaning down, he kissed her as though she was a drink of water and he was a man dying of thirst.

Later, after he made love to her again, he lay on his back and she lay with an arm over his chest, running her hand through the curly hair she found there. The curls seemed to want to capture her fingers as she caressed him.

"I hate to bring our little sojourn to an end, but we must check out and have breakfast before we start back to our claim."

She closed her eyes and sighed. He had fulfilled all her dreams of what being married should be and had granted every wish except one. He wasn't in love with her.

Considering the spontaneous decision to come to the Yukon had forced him into a marriage he didn't want, just so she'd be safer, didn't escape her mind. And he didn't want children, but she wanted a dozen. Or at least, one. What if she didn't become pregnant? Ever? Or what if she did and Barnaby couldn't handle the thought of another child?

She dressed and packed without even realizing it, as if her body knew what to do.

"Are you ready? Everything packed?" asked Barnaby.

"I think so." She looked around the room, making sure nothing was getting left behind. "I don't see anything left, so we can go now."

"We'll stop and give Kitty the key, then eat breakfast and go get the mattresses you want. They will make a great deal of difference come winter when the snow is so deep that even near the river it comes up to my knees. Wood is harder to get then because the snow is so deep. Dragging a log through the deep snow is very difficult. With that in mind, I'll be taking time now to cut some trees and chop them for firewood this winter. That's what the extra tarp is for. John bought it instead of a tent, just for that purpose. Thanks to your father, we came as prepared as we could get. He thought of almost everything."

Everything except getting buried in an avalanche and leaving me alone. Oh, Daddy. I miss you.

They stopped at the front desk where Kitty stood. She had a big smile on her face. "So, what did you two think of my honeymoon suite?"

"It's beautiful, Kitty. Thank you for giving it to us." The woman had been extremely kind since Barnaby had only asked for a room.

"I wanted to know if any couples we get would be interested in renting a suite instead of a room."

Sadie nodded. "I think any woman would love it, and to be pampered with the bath that was wonderful, too."

Kitty frowned. "The bath was extra. I hope you know that."

Sadie shook her head and waved a hand in front of her. "Of course. I'm just saying how nice it was. You should ask everyone if they would like to add a bath. I'm sure you'd sell more. Especially here, considering what the weather is like outside."

Putting an index finger to her chin, Kitty nodded. "You're right, but I can't do that for every room. I don't have enough tubs or buckets for the water. Not to mention, the stove can only handle four buckets at a time."

"What do we owe you for the night?" asked Barnaby.

"Nine dollars. Five for the room and two each for the baths," replied Kitty. "I'm giving you a discount, since you were my guinea pigs."

"Cheap at twice the price." Sadie opened her reticule and pulled out a ten-dollar bill.

Kitty gave her back a dollar. "I hope you'll come again."

"Definitely." Barnaby placed an arm around Sadie's shoulders. "The next time we come to town, hopefully we'll get the same room." He winked at Sadie. "It has a special meaning for us."

Sadie's face heated. She wouldn't have been surprised if she were as red as a ripe apple.

Barnaby laughed and steered her away from the desk before Kitty could comment. He walked them to the restaurant next door for breakfast.

After a filling breakfast of oatmeal, toasted bread with Saskatoon jam and coffee, Barnaby pointed toward the door.

"Let's get the mattresses and get back to camp."

"I'm ready." She put her napkin on the table and stood, stepping away from the table and waiting to feel Barnaby's hand on the back of her waist. Today, though, he took her hand and walked in front of her.

She wasn't sure what to make of his change. Was it because they'd made love? There had to be more to it than that. And if she found herself expecting would he change his mind about children? What then? With nothing to do about it, would he accept the baby and her, or would he reject them both?

* * *

SADIE FELT on top of the world. Barnaby made love to her and had taken great care of her since she was a virgin. Though reaching twenty-seven-years-old and still being a virgin, was something she hadn't thought possible. She had always expected she'd be married and with children by now.

Maybe her father had sheltered her too much before he went prospecting for gold, leaving her alone. But, even then, she hadn't had any serious suitors. She was neither shy nor submissive, and most men hadn't liked that.

She was more than willing to put in a full day's work beside Barnaby in the river. Even he'd had to admit she was meticulous about panning for gold. She kept even the smallest flake, and he had to admit her flakes and small nuggets were adding up. Their bag of gold was becoming heavier and heavier. He'd told her he wanted to get it weighed when they were in Dawson City, but he decided against it. He'd seen no need to let anyone know how much they had. Claim jumpers were already causing them enough trouble up and down the river, with Homer Grimes being the worst of them. According to Barnaby, if it wasn't nailed down, Grimes would steal it.

When they arrived back at the claim, Barnaby took her arm and stopped her from entering the tent. Then he put a finger over his lips. He pointed down, and she saw strange footprints around the tent and going in and out of it. *Claim jumpers.*

He pulled his pistol and then opened the tent flaps. "It's clear." He holstered his gun.

They took stock of their belongings.

"They took a bucket, a blanket, and the rest of our crystalized eggs. They might have taken some sugar and flour, but I'm not sure. Thankfully, we had all the guns with us. It doesn't look like they took any ammunition because the footlockers are undisturbed." Sadie sat on her cot. "Why can't these men just leave us alone? We haven't done anything to them."

Barnaby sat next to her and put his arm around her shoulders. "Because they have gold fever, but not the drive to do it themselves. It doesn't matter to them they're taking what isn't theirs. I suspect they go from claim to claim taking things because they've run out. Undoubtedly because they managed them poorly and didn't have the money to replace them. They thought they could just pick up gold nuggets off the land. When they found out that wasn't the case, they turned to claim jumping, looking for one that's paying out. Now, let's get those mattresses off the sled, feed Lucky and get in some time panning."

"Okay."

A WEEK after their return from town, Barnaby thought he'd seen Grimes watching the camp, but he couldn't be sure. If anyone was in the trees, they had hidden themselves well...but he didn't like the feeling he'd had.

At supper that night, he spoke up. "Sadie, we're running short of meat. I need to go hunting tomorrow. Will you be all right here on the claim by yourself?"

"Just leave me the pistol and the shotgun and I'll be fine. No claim jumper will have an easy time with me."

She was so sure of her skills.

He smiled, and then it faded as though it had never creased his face. "I want you to be vigilant for claim jumpers, especially Homer Grimes. He knows you're a woman. Most of the miners up here now do, but don't expect any help from any of them. They won't want to get involved."

"I'll be fine. You've taught me how to shoot, and I can fight, too. No one will get our claim as long as I'm here. Homer Grimes be damned."

"Good. Let's get to bed." He brought the lantern from the table to the cots and undressed down to his long johns.

Sadie sat on the side of her cot without turning it down to sleep. "Barnaby, can we...perhaps...maybe...put the mattresses on the floor and sleep together? Maybe?"

He went to her and took both of her hands in his. "Are you asking me to make love to you?"

How could she ask him? What if he didn't want to?

She looked at her boots and kept her head down, then nodded.

"You don't need to be shy with me. I'm your husband and I want to make love to you as often as you'll let me."

Sadie lifted her head. "I want you. Please, Barnaby, make love to me."

"With pleasure, *mo ghra*, with pleasure."

Barnaby pulled off the blankets and lifted the mattress from his cot, laying it on the floor.

Sadie did the same with her blankets and mattress. Then she spread all the blankets on the mattresses. They would certainly keep warm tonight.

When everything was ready, she stripped out of her clothes. She left the cotton blanket from her cot on the bottom to use as a sheet, then pulled back the blankets and crawled beneath them.

She shivered and pulled the blankets up under her chin. "It's cold in here."

"I'll put more wood in the stove. It'll warm up in no time." He walked over to the stove, opened the door and placed a good-sized piece of wood inside. Then he returned to her. "Until then, we can lay together under the blankets. I hope we can sleep this way every night."

She widened her eyes. "You do? I didn't think you wanted to since you hadn't mentioned anything."

He smiled, removed his clothes, and got under the covers with her. Then he pulled her close and wrapped her in his arms. "I was waiting until you were ready. I didn't want to push you into something you weren't prepared for."

"I'm ready."

"We don't have to rush things. Let's just be together and enjoy touching each other. Then, when the tent warms up, we can make love."

It didn't take long for the tent to warm and the covers to seem like too much.

Sadie threw back her blankets. "Now, I'm hot under them."

"So am I." He pushed the coverings to the bottom of the bed, then sat back on his heels and gazed at her. "You're beautiful. I think you're the loveliest woman I've ever known."

She smiled and then lowered her gaze. "You know, I appreciate the flattery, but I'm trying very hard not to cover up with my arms. I know you've seen all of me before, but that doesn't prevent me from being shy about you looking at me."

"Thank you for not hiding yourself from me. It would be a shame to keep all this beauty covered up."

"I have to say, you are the most well-formed man I've ever known, and I enjoy looking at you."

He threw his head back and laughed. Then he leaned forward. "I'm the only man you've ever known, so I'd have to be the most *well-formed*."

She giggled and then laughed along with him. "I guess that *was* a pretty ridiculous thing to say."

He stopped laughing and gazed into her eyes. "I'm glad you find me pleasing to look at." He leaned down and kissed her, their mouths melding and becoming as if they were one.

She was tentative to begin with. Then she relaxed into the kiss, wrapped her arms around his neck and brought him closer to her. He was almost lying upon her but took most of his weight on his arms, even as he lay more fully upon her.

And then he loved her, leaving her panting and

feeling drugged by his lovemaking. She was relaxed and more content than she'd ever felt before. She cuddled into his side and lay her hand across his massive chest. "What time are you leaving in the morning?"

"At sunup."

"Wake me and I'll fix your breakfast."

"It's not necessary. I have some hardtack and jerky from our last trip to Dawson City. Those will do me until I get home. But I warn you, I'll be hungry when I return."

"Any idea what time that will be?" She ran her fingers through the hair on his chest. The silky strands tried to trap her fingers.

"That depends on how lucky I am. I'll be aiming for deer. A nice-sized doe would be perfect. I could field dress it and carry it home. If I get an elk, it will take me about four trips to get it all back here, and that's assuming the animals don't take it all first."

"Is that likely?"

He shrugged and covered her hand with one of his. "The bears are awake and looking for any free meal, building fat for their next hibernation. The mountain lions will take what they can, then wolf packs will want their share. How close I am to camp will determine whether I go back for the rest of the animal or not. If it's an elk, I'll butcher it in place and carry as much of the meat, not the bone, as I can in my backpack."

"So the likelihood of you returning to the animal is not high."

"Unfortunately, that's correct."

She sighed. "That's too bad. But at least the meat doesn't go to waste."

"Yes, it will get eaten. Not much goes to waste in this wilderness."

"You should get some rest. Morning will be here before we know it."

He pulled her up his body. "Mmhm." He kissed her.

Sadie felt herself being enthralled by him, and when he turned her to her back, and she let him.

"Say no now if you don't want this as much as I do."

"Yes."

He groaned, and then he made sweet, passionate love to her.

When morning came, Sadie didn't feel like she'd slept at all. Barnaby had made love to her twice more in the night. She might be tired now, but last night he'd invigorated her. She had gone and fallen in love with her husband. But that was impossible. How could she love a man who didn't want children?

CHAPTER 8

*S*adie watched Barnaby head out for his hunt with her new rifle and wearing an empty backpack. If he got an animal, a lot of work would need to be done to prepare it for storage. They would have to smoke it or dry it or something. They couldn't eat that much fresh meat. Could they? Barnaby had an enormous appetite that their meals could never fill, even though she tried to make extra.

She couldn't dwell on what Barnaby's hunting trip would bring. She had gold to discover. Despite the warm late June weather, she dressed in the same clothes, including her long johns, wool pants, shirt and last but not least, her pistol. Since she would be in the river, she wanted to be warm and to keep as clean as possible. Panning for gold was dirty work. Even though she and Barnaby both washed every day, she looked forward to their now once a month trip to

Dawson City and a decent bath. Now that they were truly married, she wasn't so shy around him.

Barnaby had been gone most of the day. Despite it being past lunchtime, she had skipped the meal since she wasn't hungry and opted to continue working.

Sadie kept her head down, searching for the elusive shiny gold nuggets and flakes. She'd found a big nugget...almost the size of her thumb. It would more than pay for their night at Kitty's and then some, assuming they didn't use her cash. Out of nowhere, she heard a harsh voice from behind her.

"Well, if it isn't Sadie Drake and here all alone, too."

She dropped her pan and turned with her hand on her pistol. Homer Grimes stood on the bank. His hair was dirtier than the last time she saw him, if that was possible. He had a pistol in his right hand, aimed at her.

"Don't you be thinking of going for the hog leg on your hip. I'd kill you before you got it out of the holster."

She believed him and raised both of her hands. "What do you want, Homer? Money? I've got some gold from today. A nice nugget, too. I'll give it to you. Just go away, back to your hidey hole."

"Oh, I'll be goin' back, but you and I have some business first. Get on up here and don't think of doin' nothin' fast. You just take your time and come easy like. You're gonna enjoy what I have in mind."

"I doubt you have anything that would give me enjoyment. Not after Barnaby."

Grimes' face reddened, and he snarled, "Get up here and go to your tent. Real careful."

She walked out of the river, never taking her gaze off of Grimes. "I'm not going in that tent unless you're leaving."

"I'm not leaving, girly, and you will go in that tent. Now!" He waved the pistol at her. "Unless you'd like Barnaby to find you with a hole in you."

"I'll go." *If I can get to the shotgun before he comes inside...it's right by the opening to the tent, but I don't know if I'm fast enough.* She walked, head held high and back straight, to the tent and bent down to enter. It took all her willpower not to shake like a leaf, but she wouldn't give him her fear to hold over her. Her stomach cramped and she thought she'd vomit. But she kept her head up and swallowed hard.

Grimes poked her in the back with his gun. "Get in there, don't dawdle." He pushed her into the tent.

She fell onto her knees and couldn't grab the shotgun.

He followed her inside and stood by the opening. 'Get your clothes off. Now!" He didn't wave the gun this time, but kept it steady and aimed at her.

She stood and slipped off her suspenders, then slowly unbuttoned her shirt and removed it. Sadie stood in the middle of her and Barnaby's bed with her muddy boots, but she didn't care right now. She had to distract Grimes. "Homer, why are you doing this? You know Barnaby will kill you. You can't run far enough where he won't find you."

"He's got to catch me first. Now, shut up and do as yer told."

She dropped her shirt on the mattress at her feet. Then she unbuttoned her pants. "I have to take off my boots to get my pants off."

He stood with his legs apart enough to keep him steady. "Then do it quick like."

She saw he was nervous.

He kept looking behind him, like he was watching for Barnaby.

Sadie was afraid he'd shoot her, but she wasn't about to let him rape her, either. She'd rather die. She took off her right boot, but instead of setting it by the bed, she threw it at him. It hit his gun which went off as it fell out of his hand, shooting a hole in the back of the tent. She lunged on her knees to grab his gun and then turned to her back and aimed toward him.

He fell on her, trying to force her to relinquish the weapon.

She pulled the trigger.

He howled. It hit him on the foot. He backhanded her and then punched her in the face.

Sadie heard the bones crack and pain shoot through her face, but she didn't stop fighting. She clawed at him, felt his cheek beneath her fingers and dug deep into the soft tissue and felt the blood run over her fingers and down his face.

He hit her again.

She ran out of cheek and let go of his face as she fisted her hands and hit at him as hard as she could.

She connected with his face. Her hand slid on his blood over his cheek to his nose.

He howled. "You filthy bi—"

She hit him with her left fist, not as hard as she wanted but enough to push him away.

He howled, grabbed his nose, got up and ran as fast as he could out of the tent.

By the time she got out of the tent, he'd headed up the river. She shot at him but missed. He was too far away.

She walked back into the tent and got a washcloth from in the dirty clothes. No sense in bleeding on a clean one.

She fixed her pants, unlaced her left boot and changed socks. Her boots were too precious to foul them with a muddy sock. Then she put her boots back on, the socks in the dirty clothes and went out to the river. She dipped her gold pan into the cold, clear water and cleaned it out. Then she took the pan with clean water back to the tent, sat by the firepit and, after stopping the bleeding, she washed as well as she could.

Barnaby would notice, but there wasn't a thing she could do about that. She'd won. She wasn't raped, and a broken nose was a little price to pay to keep that from happening.

* * *

Barnaby headed home in the early afternoon. As he walked through the forest, he whistled. He'd had the best day. He'd gotten the good-sized doe before noon, he'd butcher it on the spot. His backpack was full of meat and he'd be home in time to make love to Sadie before supper. He whistled until he got to the claim.

When he arrived back at camp, he expected to see Sadie at the river or baking bread. Neither was true. He opened the tent flap and found her sitting at the table, holding a washcloth to her face.

He smiled. She wanted to be clean for him.

She turned his way.

The air in his lungs whooshed out in one long breath. "What the hell happened?"

She turned away. "Homer Grimes is what. He tried to rape me. I had something to say about that. He'll be nursing his foot where I shot him. Well, the gun shot him, but I tried to."

Barnaby regained his breath and walked over, falling to his knees. "Let me see." He took her chin gently between a thumb and forefinger and turned her to face him.

"Oh, baby, I'm so sorry. I should never have left you alone. I should have known better."

"No!" Her voice softened. "You prepared me as best you could, and that preparation saved my life. I will be forever grateful for that." She reached over and cupped his face. "Besides, you can't be with me twenty-four hours a day. But you're here now and that's what matters." Reaching up with the hand that had been on his face, she touched her nose and winced. "I'll be ugly for a while and maybe forever with this broken nose."

"If you want, I can fix it for you. It will hurt, but should feel better afterward. I won't do anything you don't wish me to."

"Is it that crooked?"

"Not bad really."

"I think I'll just leave it. I might have a crooked nose, but as long as you don't mind it, neither do I."

"Okay, why don't you lie down for a while? You look like you could use some rest. In the meantime, I'll be looking for Homer Grimes."

"He's probably long gone." She laid on the mattresses on the muddy blanket.

"Get under the covers. I'll take that blanket outside. We can clean it later."

* * *

SHE SAT up and took off her boots, then got a clean washcloth for her nose which had started bleeding again, before getting under the blankets.

After about ten minutes, the bleeding stopped, but she felt exhausted. Like she'd worked the entire day without a break. And her body hurt from fighting with Grimes. But she'd take this kind of hurting every day compared to what Grimes had in store.

Barnaby came inside. "Is there anything I can do for you before I go?"

She sat up, leaning back, arms straight and her hands flat on the mattress. "No. I'm fine." She pointed at the weapon in the corner of the tent. "I'd like the shotgun next to me. I don't intend to get caught by anyone else."

"Of course." He reached over and grabbed the shotgun, then placed it next to her on the bed. He fell to his knees beside her. "After I get done with Grimes, no one will bother you...ever."

She touched his arm. "Don't kill him. I don't want you to go to prison for killing him." *Even if Grimes deserves to be dead.*

He patted her hand where it lay on his arm. "I'll try not to." He leaned over and kissed her forehead. "If you can, nap until I return. I shouldn't be long. I don't imagine he has gotten very far on that leg. Besides, tracking him will be easy now."

"I don't know. He moved fast enough to get out of here before I shot him again."

"As well he should. Now, go to sleep. I'll wake you when I return. I promise I won't be gone long." He kissed the top of her head and left the tent.

Sadie doubted she would sleep, but her eyes seemed to close regardless of what she thought or wanted. She finally gave in to the need and closed her eyes.

She awoke to the smell of food cooking. It smelled good, like meat frying. She sat up and her head started pounding. Lying down again, she closed her eyes and put a palm on her forehead. "Oh, God, I hurt."

"Shh. I made you some willow bark tea."

Sadie took the cup of tea and drank as though she hadn't had a drink in years. The tea was cool and eased the dryness in her mouth and throat. She looked up at

Barnaby and smiled. "Thank you. I don't think I've ever felt this bad. Did you find Grimes?"

Barnaby's mouth set in a firm line, and he shook his head. "No. His tent was empty and the miners on either side claimed not to have seen him today. That might be true. He might have a camp in the trees so he could watch us. It wasn't by accident that he found you alone. He's been watching, waiting for me to leave. And he's cleverer than I thought. I lost his tracks when they entered the river."

"If I'd had time to think about it, I would agree. He came up behind me, not from either side."

Barnaby nodded. "That makes sense. He is likely behind us somewhere in the forest. But it's too big for me to search. I'll have to wait and keep an eye out when we go to Dawson City. He'll go there. He'll have to, eventually, since he's been shot."

Sadie finished the tea and handed the cup to Barnaby. "I think I feel better, and I'd like to get up and sit at the table. This is warm and cozy, but I'd rather sit with you."

He smiled. "I'd like that. Dinner is almost done. I've fried up a couple of venison steaks." He moved back to the stove and turned over the steaks.

"What's venison? I thought you were after deer."

"A deer is the animal. After it's been butchered, the meat is called venison. It's the same with an elk."

"Do they taste the same?"

"They are similar, but there are differences. In my experience, elk venison is a milder meat. Deer venison has a little, very little, stronger flavor. But you'll like this, anyway." He waggled his eyebrows and then took the skillet off the stove.

She walked over to the table. The place settings were already down. Two metal plates, metal cups and, of course, the utensils. Metal was sturdier. It didn't break. You could heat food directly in it with no pan.

Barnaby put a steak on her plate and two on his. He had half a loaf of sourdough bread on the table, too.

Sadie cut off a bite of the steak and put it in her mouth. Uncertain about the intended taste, the flavor proved quite mild. "This is good. I like it." She reached for the bread, just as Barnaby did.

He laughed. "After you. Might not be any left once I get hold of it."

She shook her head and with a laugh tore off a chunk. "Is this the last loaf?"

"It is. Looks like tomorrow, if you're feeling up to it, will be a baking day."

"I'll be fine. I just need some more rest, and I'll be right as rain." Suddenly, a thought struck her. "What month is this?"

He closed his eyes and furrowed his brows. "It's late August. You arrived at the end of March. Why?"

Five months! I haven't had my menses in three months. May was the last one. I think we first made love the middle of June. I'm pregnant. Two-and-a-half months pregnant. I knew it could happen, but didn't think it would be so soon. I'd hoped I'd be able to get Barnaby to warm to the idea. Now, he still doesn't want children, but this situation is as

111

much his fault as mine. We'll have to figure it out togeth-er...as soon as I get the nerve to tell him. "No reason. I just couldn't remember. When does the first snow come?"

"Mid-September, usually. Is there a particular reason you're interested in the first snow of the season?"

She shook her head and cut another bite of the meat. "No reason. Just curious, that's all." She put the bite in her mouth and chewed. Her mind was going a mile a minute. Would he know before she told him? Her knowledge of signs came from watching her neighbor Lacey's mother during her pregnancy. She got sick in the mornings for a while, and then Lacey told her that her mother wanted strange things to eat at all hours of the day and night. Her poor father was in a dither for the six months he knew about the baby to come.

"You're quiet tonight. Are you in pain? Would you like some more willow bark tea?"

She smiled, pleased he was being so attentive. "Actually, I'd love another cup of tea."

He rose and put the water pail back on the stove. "It just needs to get a little hotter. It shouldn't be too long."

"I'm not worried about it."

Barnaby sat again, reached across the table, and took her hand. "What's really bothering you?"

She took her hand back and then clasped her hands together in her lap. She looked down at the table and then back up at him. "I'm pregnant. I know you don't want children, but we're having one, despite your desires. If you truly don't want it, you don't have to have anything to do with it. I'll raise the child on my own."

His mouth formed a grim line. "This was bound to happen, someday. I hadn't expected it so soon. I'd hoped I would accept the idea before this happened, but I haven't. I'm going out. I need some air. The willow bark is in your cup. Just pour the hot water over it and let it steep for about five minutes." He stood, grabbed his hat off his cot and left.

He didn't stomp out as she expected him to, but he hadn't kissed her goodbye, either.

Tears formed of their own accord. If she'd had her way, she wouldn't cry, but that didn't seem possible. Her marriage seemed to be falling apart, all because of a wonderful, blessed event. The birth of a child. She would not regret that she was expecting, and she wouldn't ever be anything but happy and grateful for this consequence of making love to her husband. If only she could convince him. This was a joyous occasion. But convincing him would be harder than it should be. Just how hard she didn't know.

CHAPTER 9

Sadie was already in bed by the time Barnaby returned. He stripped out of his clothes and crawled into bed.

She shivered as he took the warmth of the blankets while he covered them both.

He gathered her into his arms.

His heated skin warmed her.

He kissed her temple. "I'm sorry, *mo ghra*. I never meant to hurt you."

Tears came unbidden; she couldn't stop them. "I wanted you to be happy. Even though I knew that was unlikely...I hoped."

"I will try. That is all I can do. I worry this child will be like my first son and die while still a baby."

She sniffled and swallowed over a lump in her throat. "We'll pray that doesn't happen."

He pulled her closer, though she didn't think that was possible.

She turned and pillowed her head on his chest, her left arm holding his waist. She loved him. Had she always been in love with him? She agreed to the marriage because she was attracted to him, regardless of what he said. But she'd wanted him all to herself. She didn't want him visiting whorehouses anymore. And, to the best of her knowledge, he had not. He was faithful, as was she. Though she knew no one would or could compare with her gentle giant, she found herself thinking of the men she'd known in Missouri. They were thin and pale in comparison.

With a quickness she wouldn't have expected from such a big man, he turned them, so he was on top, braced on his elbows so as not to crush her. Then he made love to her. They had never made love so tenderly before. He was careful of her injuries and when he kissed her, was extra gentle. This love making and the care he took of her, she thought this was what pure love was supposed to be.

WHEN SADIE AWOKE, Barnaby was gone. She heard him outside washing his face and hands, getting ready for the day. She rushed to dress after getting out from under the warm blankets. The air was too cold to stay in the buff for very long.

Once dressed, she built the fire in the stove and heated yesterday's coffee. Each time she bent over, her face hurt. Not just her nose, but her cheeks and forehead. She also had a headache and her eyes felt swollen. She was a mess, but she had work to do and couldn't be lying around all day.

So, she started breakfast. Today was oatmeal and a couple of venison steaks. She needed to bake today. The bread was one of their staples and made their sometimes-meager meals palatable. She wished she had butter to go with it, and they were down to their last bit of jam. They needed to venture to Dawson City for supplies and to locate a doctor who could confirm her pregnancy.

She finished the oatmeal, and the coffee was hot. Stepping out of the tent, she gazed around for Barnaby. "Breakfast is ready."

He entered the tent a few minutes later, a grin on his face. "How are you this fine morning, *mo ghra*?"

Sadie liked his nickname. "What does *mo ghra* mean?"

"It is Gaelic for beloved."

Her mouth dropped open and then a smile split her face. "I'm your beloved?"

"You are. You're my wife and soon to be the mother of my child."

The smile remained on his face even when he talked of the child. Had last night convinced him he should be happy about the baby? She wanted to know, but she was afraid to ask.

She watched as he came over to the table where she had dished up their breakfast. "It's time for us to make a trip to Dawson City. We need flour, sugar, oatmeal, crystalized eggs, if we can find them, and even more bacon would be nice."

He sat across from her. "You know, your money makes our life here much nicer than it would otherwise be."

"I know. I'm...we're...fortunate and it's almost gone. I hate leaving the claim. Do you suppose we could get our neighbor, Seth Jones, to watch it in exchange for some bread and meat? I'm sure he would enjoy the extra food."

Their neighbor, Seth Jones, had the claim to the south of theirs. Whatever they missed as far as gold, he would have the right to it if he found it.

"I don't know, but I'll ask him. Perhaps we can bring him back some supplies and save him a trip."

"Yes, besides the bread and meat. I doubt he had gone hunting since he hurt his leg, so he might enjoy having the venison more than anything."

"I'll check as soon as I see him outside."

She gave him a peck on the cheek. "Thank you."

The middle of the river flowed fast and deep. Barnaby, because of his size, was better able to work out there. But even at that, they found most of the gold outside of the center toward the banks, which was just fine with Sadie.

Today, though, she would bake, and she loved baking days. She stayed warm and dry, which suited her just fine, but she would never complain to Barnaby about working the river. She was as much a partner in this venture as he was, and they put all their gold into one bag.

Supper that night was fresh sourdough bread and venison stew. Barnaby had taught her to recognize wild burdock root, which she gathered to put into the stew. Burdock root was harsh if not soaked in water for five or ten minutes before cooking. After soaking, she sliced the burdock and added it to the broth made from frying the meat in lard. It wasn't the best stew, but it was different and with the bread, the dish was filling. Anything to make their meals less bland.

"What did Seth say?"

"He'd be glad to." He dunked the last of his bread in the stew. "He wants us to bring him back some of the crystallized eggs, if we find any. And he'd love to have the bread and the meat."

"Wonderful. I made three loaves of bread. You can take the food to him after supper. Let's go tomorrow and plan on spending the night. I'd like to sleep in a proper bed again."

"Me, too. But as long as you're beside me, I always have a proper bed." He waggled his brows.

She laughed and pointed. "You're a wicked man, Barnaby Drake."

"Only with you, *mo ghra*. Only with you." He stood. "I'll gather the bread and the meat and take it to Sam. Be right back."

After he returned that night, Barnaby made love to

her twice before letting her get some rest. They would both need it for the trip to Dawson City. The journey was over rough terrain, walking with Lucky. She appreciated now how blessed she'd been to get Lucky here.

The next morning, after breakfast at dawn, they headed out, arriving in Dawson City around noon. They left Lucky at the stables by the Mountie station.

Her stomach rumbled. "I'm starving."

Barnaby reached for her hand and then tucked it in the crook of his elbow. "So am I, but let's check in with Kitty first and see if she has a room available."

"Okay."

As they walked into Kitty's hotel, she glanced up from the desk.

She frowned. "What in the world happened to you, Sadie?" She turned on Barnaby. "You better not have done this, and I hope you killed the man who did."

"I will if I ever find him," growled Barnaby. "Have you seen Homer Grimes?"

Kitty snorted. "That reprobate? He doesn't have the nerve to come in here after what he did. Beat up one of my girls. I don't go for that. Any man that has to beat up a woman, is no man and not welcome in my place." She leaned on the tall desk. "Now, what can I do for you?"

Barnaby took Sadie's hand and kissed the top. "We'd like a room for the night, if you have one available."

Kitty glanced at the cubbyholes on the wall behind her. "Looks like the only one available is the suite you had last time. Folks just don't seem to want to pay extra for the bigger room."

He looked at Sadie. "What do you say? Want the honeymoon suite again?"

She thought about the comfort of the room they had already enjoyed once and grinned. "I'd love it and the bath, too."

Smiling, he gave her hand a squeeze and turned his gaze toward Kitty. "We'll take it and two baths, just like last time."

"Okay." Kitty smiled widely. "Just sign here." She turned the register around for him to sign. Then she grabbed the key out of its hole in the wall. "Here's the key. You know the way."

"Sounds great. We'll get something to eat and then we'll stop by and let you know we're ready for the baths."

"Sounds good. I'll wait to hear from you before I order them."

He took the key and led them down the hall, then opened the door and let Sadie enter first. Then he followed her in and set his backpack on the floor near the door. "Are you ready to get something to eat?"

Sadie's stomach rumbled again. She laughed and held her belly. "Yes, I'm definitely ready."

He chuckled and held out his arm. "Shall we?"

She placed a hand in the crook of his elbow. "We shall."

They walked next door to the restaurant and were shown to a table in the middle of the room.

Barnaby held out her chair and then seated himself. He placed a hand palm up on the table.

Sadie smiled and placed a hand on his. "You're being so romantic...first walking me here and now holding hands on the table. Should I be expecting something?"

Barnaby rubbed circles on the inside of her wrist.

She shivered and her heart beat faster.

"Can't a husband hold hands with his wife?"

Smiling, she shook her head. "It's usually not done in public."

"Do you see anything *usual* about Dawson City or the people in it?"

Sadie glanced around. All the tables were full of men. Miners or claim jumpers, but she couldn't tell the difference. "You're right. Nothing about Dawson City is the least bit normal compared to St. Louis society."

"After dinner, and our baths, we'll have a peaceful time in bed without blankets weighing us down. I can turn over and make love to you much easier." He waggled his eyebrows.

Sadie laughed, but it filled her stomach with butter-flies, and her insides heated at his words.

Sally came and took their order for the special of the day, elk steak with biscuits and cream gravy.

Barnaby ordered two meals as usual.

Sadie ordered one and then only ate half. Her reduced appetite surprised her, but maybe she was just excited to be there. Getting a bath and sleeping in a proper bed always made such a difference.

He ate the rest.

When Barnaby finished, he paid Sally and then escorted Sadie back to their room with a stop at the front desk to order their baths.

At the room, he opened the door, stood back for her to enter first, and then stood there. "I have to run a quick errand. I'll be right back." He leaned down and kissed her before shutting the door.

* * *

BARNABY HURRIED down to the mercantile. Last time he was there, he'd noticed some gold wedding bands. He walked inside and directly to the case with the rings.

"Well, hi Barnaby. What can I do for you today? Need supplies already?"

"No, Joe, I need a wedding band for my wife."

Joe smiled. "Let me show you what I've got." He pulled out a tray of gold rings. Thick ones, thin ones, engraved ones.

Barnaby didn't have a lot of money, but he'd brought some gold. He already knew that Joe had scales, and he was honest with what he paid. "I'd like one of those thin ones." He grinned. "I'll get her a diamond one when we hit the big one."

"Sounds good." Joe unlocked the case and brought out the tray of rings. "Do you know what size she wears?"

Barnaby's eyes widened for a moment. "Well, I figure if I get it to fit to the first knuckle on my little finger, that should fit her. If it doesn't we'll come back tomorrow and get the right size. Will that work?"

"Sure thing. You staying at Kitty's?"

"No place else in this town I trust, and she has the nicest rooms."

Joe handed Barnaby the ring. "I don't have any boxes or I'd give you one. That's twenty dollars even."

Barnaby put the ring in a pants pocket and pulled out his poke from another. He took out a small nugget. Added to his fifteen dollars, that should be enough. He set the money and the nugget on the counter. "Will this do it or do you need more?"

"Come on over to the scales and we'll see what we have." Joe walked out from behind the jewelry counter and walked to the next counter along the back wall. "Now let's see." He put the nugget on one side of the scales and different sized weights until the two sides balanced. "Looks like I owe you a dollar." Joe reached under the counter and took out his cash box. He unlocked it and handed Barnaby a one-dollar bill.

"Thanks Joe. I hope it fits and we don't see you tomorrow."

Joe laughed. "Always a pleasure, my friend."

Barnaby headed back to the hotel. He stopped at the desk and checked on their baths, then walked back to the room.

He knocked before using the key to enter.

* * *

As soon as he closed the door, she was in his arms, his lips on hers.

With just his lips, he made her melt in all the right places.

"Sadie." He moaned.

"Oh, Barnaby, make love to me."

He kissed her neck. "Soon, *mo cuishle*, soon, my darling. After we bathe."

About that time, the men came to the door with the baths.

Once they were gone, Sadie slowly undressed. Her stomach was slightly rounded with their child.

Barnaby stared. "Even in pregnancy, you are the most exquisite woman I've ever seen. And I'm your husband. I get to see you as often as I want."

Her face heated, and she filled with pleasure at his compliment.

Barnaby undressed and climbed into his tub.

Sadie climbed into her tub and dunked herself into the water and wet her hair. Then she picked up the bar of soap provided by the hotel and rubbed it all over her head before dropping the soap beside the tub. She added water to her hair and then scrubbed her scalp and made enough suds to wash it down the length to the end. After she was done, she laid back in the water and rinsed as much of the soap out as possible. She washed her body and her privates.

Barnaby finished before her and stood with a towel wrapped low on his hips.

"Will you rinse me, please?"

"Sure." He grabbed the extra bucket of warm water. She stood.

He poured the water slowly over the top of her head.

She worked the suds out of her hair and rubbed her body to remove the last remnants of soap.

He set down the bucket and handed her a towel.

She wrapped it around her head.

Then she stepped out of the tub and he gave her a second towel, which she used to dry her body. She looked up at him. "I didn't bring a nightgown. I guess you'll just have to keep me warm."

He chuckled. "Don't I always?"

She smiled seductively, lowered her lashes and then slowly raked his body with her gaze. "That you do."

Laughing, Barnaby picked her up and carried her to the bed. "Before we finish this wonderful conversation with some activity I know we'll both like, I have something for you." He rose and took something from his pants. He sat back on the bed. "Sadie Drake, will you marry me?"

She chuckled and swatted his chest. "We're already married, silly."

He took her left hand and placed the ring on her finger. Then he kissed it and kissed her.

She held up her hand and admired the thin gold band. It fit a little snug but that was perfect. She wouldn't lose it in the river. "Oh, Barnaby, it's beautiful and perfect. I love y…it. I love it so much." She leaned over, pushed him back on the pillows and then showed him how much she appreciated the ring.

Oh, he kept her warm and then some.

CHAPTER 10

They made love in the hotel bed all afternoon until suppertime.

"Come on and get dressed. I'm starving." He rolled to the side and sat up as he placed his feet on the floor.

Sadie felt like a rag doll, but she rose from the bed, freshened her private parts, and dressed in clean clothes. Once she brushed her hair and gently wiped a wet washcloth over her face, she felt better.

"You know I'm hungry myself." Her stomach rumbled.

Barnaby laughed. "I guess you are." He waited until she was near the door before he opened it and ushered her through the opening.

They stopped at the desk and asked for the tubs to be removed.

Supper was roasted elk with gravy, mashed potatoes and sourdough bread. The meal was filling, if not inventive.

After they finished supper, she wrapped her hand through the crook in his elbow while they walked down the boardwalk. Though it was past eight at night, it was still very much daylight. They walked along past ramshackle buildings of varying degrees of finish. Some were painted while others were bare wood.

Sadie was amazed when she looked at the windows. She couldn't imagine bringing glass over the mountains, but some buildings had glass windows. Others had only shutters which were open now to provide air circulation. She imagined in winter they would remain closed until the spring thaw.

"Do you know if the doctor would be open now? I don't want to wait until tomorrow morning to have him confirm that I'm expecting."

"I don't know. Shall we walk that way? We need to check on Lucky, anyway, and they are in the same general direction."

She cocked her head and smiled at him. Suddenly, she wanted to kiss her husband more than anything. She stopped, reached up, wrapped a hand around his neck, and brought his lips to hers. She kissed him, her mouth making love to him as much as she could there on the boardwalk.

His arms wrapped around her, and he brought her flush against him. He broke the kiss and set her away. "I'll remember this for later, I promise."

She giggled, excitement running through her as her heart pounded and her pulse raced. "I'll hold you to it."

She took his arm again, and they continued a

couple of blocks and then made a left for another block. The doctor's office was in a building that looked like a home. She supposed the doctor must live there, too. A shingle hung on a post said, *Doctor Amos Kitteridge.*

Sadie walked in front of Barnaby up the gravel path toward the house. The garden boasted flowers of all kinds, most of which were wildflowers she'd seen in the forests and flats around their claim. The doctor had a couple of rose bushes and a geranium plant, too.

The house had a wide, covered porch on the front side of the building. The house itself was a white clapboard structure with light-green shutters. The door was light-green, as well.

Barnaby took her hand when they reached the porch and knocked on the door before entering. When they crossed the threshold, the stairs were directly in front of them and to the right was a small waiting room with six wooden, straight-backed chairs, three on the same wall as the entry door. The doctor had painted the waiting room the same light green as the door and shutters, which Sadie found calming.

"Have a seat while I locate the doctor," said Barnaby. He went off down the hall to the left of the staircase that formed the fourth wall of the waiting room.

She sat in one of the wooden chairs and wondered if the room she was in was the living room at one time.

"Dr. Kitteridge!" she heard Barnaby yell.

"Coming." A man's voice emanated from the back of the house.

A few moments later, the two men appeared from the hallway.

Barnaby crossed the room to stand at her side. "Dr. Kitteridge, this is my wife, Sadie."

She stood and held out her right hand.

The doctor, an older man with graying brown hair and spectacles, clasped it in both of his. "Mrs. Drake. So nice to finally meet you. There was quite a sensation when you arrived in town. I'd heard there was a stampede." He released her hand.

"Yes, a misunderstanding on my part. I had no idea the presence of a mere woman would have such an effect. Of course, I didn't know women were in such short supply, either."

The doctor laughed. "Well, what can I do for you today?"

"My wife believes she's expecting and would like you to confirm it."

"How far along do you think you are?" asked the doctor.

Barnaby looked over at Sadie.

"A little over two months."

"That's very early. I'd prefer to wait for at least another month or two, so there is no question about what I'm feeling. A physical exam is the only way to confirm a pregnancy, but I prefer not to do them early due to other possible sensations."

"Are there any physical signs I should watch for?" asked Sadie.

"Have you been nauseous in the mornings, usually to the point of vomiting?" asked Dr. Kitteridge.

"She's not been sick in the morning. I remember that with my first wife. She couldn't keep down breakfast for a good three months."

Sadie's eyes widened. "Three months!"

Barnaby nodded. "She was *not* happy about it either."

The doctor chuckled. "No, I imagine she wasn't, but after that stopped, she was probably very happy about expecting a new life."

Barnaby gazed at Sadie. "Yes, she was."

"Well, I'm happy now and I will remain happy regardless of how sick I get. I can't imagine not being happy about expecting a baby." *I wish he wouldn't talk about his first wife. What if his feelings for me never change because he's still in love with her?*

The doctor clasped his hands in front of him. "We'll see how you feel in a month or so, after you've been having morning sickness."

"Maybe I won't get morning sickness." She gazed at the doctor with hope in her eyes. "I don't have to get it, do I?"

"No, indeed, but seventy to eighty percent of women do for one length of time or another."

Sadie's shoulders slumped. "Oh."

Barnaby placed his arm around her shoulders. "It's all right. We'll get through it together."

She peered up at him, unconvinced. "If you say so."

"Doctor," said Barnaby. "I'd also like to know if you

have had Homer Grimes as a patient? He would have had a foot wound."

The doctor frowned. "I can't talk about patients or their medical history. I'm sorry."

"That's all right. I had to ask since my wife is the one who shot him. We're on our way to see the Mounties now."

The doctor gazed at Sadie. "I'm guessing that Homer is the one who gave you those two black eyes and swollen nose."

She nodded. "Yes, sir, he is. I intend to press charges for attempted rape."

Doctor Kitteridge took her hand again. "I'm so sorry, my dear. Do you mind if I have a look at your injuries?"

"No, sir. Go ahead, but I don't know what you can do for me now. Everything is starting to heal and Barnaby doesn't care if I have a crooked nose."

"I think I'll have a look, anyway." He gently pressed on her right cheek.

Sadie pulled back. "That hurts, but not bad. I just don't like it."

"That's fine. I just wanted to see if your cheek bone was broken, but it appears to be fine. May I touch the left one?"

"Okay, I guess."

He pressed her cheek.

Sadie sucked in a breath and jerked from his touch.

He clasped his hands in front of him. "Your left cheek might be fractured, but not badly. It'll just take more time for that side to heal. I want you to drink willow bark tea before bed every night for the next two weeks. That will help with the pain. You might want to do it in the mornings as well."

"Okay, Doctor, I will." Sadie leaned into Barnaby's side.

He put an arm around her shoulders.

Next, they went down to the Mountie station. They checked on Lucky and then went inside and reported Homer Grimes for attempted rape and assault.

The Mountie at the desk took her statement. He was young, good-looking and this was probably his first assignment post. "Do you intend to press charges against this Homer Grimes?"

"Yes." Sadie had a hard time not shouting her answer at the dense man. "Why else would I report it to you?"

"I understand your frustration, Mrs. Drake, but I have to ask the question."

Barnaby huffed out a breath. "I wish when his gun went off, it had hit more than his foot."

"I'll file this and post it on the board so everyone is aware. We don't like men who beat women, regardless of what other villainy they had in mind."

"I don't either." Barnaby pulled Sadie to his side. "I will protect my wife to whatever extent is necessary."

"We understand that, Mr. Drake, but please don't take the law into your own hands."

"I won't if I don't have to. That's all I can say."

"And that's all we ask."

They left the Mountie station and headed back to the hotel for the night, where they made love until they were both ragged and then fell into an exhausted sleep.

* * *

THE NEXT MORNING, they then made all their purchases and even managed to get crystallized eggs for themselves and Seth. Then they headed back.

They'd just turned the bend when Sadie saw someone lying on the ground of their claim, next to the river. "Seth!" She started running.

Barnaby took off next to her, keeping Lucky's lead rope in his hand.

Lucky trotted behind them.

Barnaby reached the man first and turned him over. "It's not Seth, but this man is dead."

"Dead!" She looked around her in a complete circle but didn't see Seth. She hurried to their tent and looked inside, but it was empty. Then she ran down to Seth's tent.

"Sadie! Wait!" Barnaby ran behind her, his longer legs eating up the distance between them. He grabbed her hand and pulled her to a stop. "Wait. We don't know what happened here. Seth could be in there alone or he could be there with the man who killed the one we found. Just wait."

She nodded and then swiped her cheeks, fear filling her. *What if Seth is dead? What if he'd been protecting their claim when it happened? What other reason could there be for that man lying dead by the river?*

She watched Barnaby pull his revolver, carefully open the tent, and look inside.

"Sadie, come quick."

Running, she was at his side in a heartbeat. "What?"

"Seth. You tend to him while I bury our perpetrator away from the claim in the woods."

She entered the tent and saw Seth lying on his cot. He was bleeding from his side. "Seth, what happened?" She grabbed a towel and held it to his injury to stop the bleeding. "I need to clean the wound so I can see the damage."

After applying pressure for a few minutes, she wet a washcloth from the bucket of water next to his small stove. The water was still warm, like he'd been heating it before he headed out to their claim.

She went onto her knees beside the cot and unbuttoned his shirt and his long johns. Clothing was too precious to rip them. She pulled his right arm out of the both garments. Once she got a look at the wound from the front, she rolled him so she could check his back. He had a larger wound on his back, showing the bullet had gone through and wasn't lodged anywhere in his body.

"Seth. Can you hear me?" She patted his face. "Come on, Seth. Wake up."

He groaned and opened his eyes. "Sadie?" He tried to sit up. "Danger. Claim jumpers."

She placed a hand on his shoulder to keep him from

moving too much. "It's okay. Barnaby is here. He's burying the body of the man you killed. Were there more of them?"

Seth's eyes widened.

A hand wearing a dirty leather glove covered Sadie's mouth from behind.

She tried to scream and tried to pull the hand from her mouth.

The hand didn't budge.

It pulled her backwards through the opening in the tent.

She fought, tugging at his hand, digging her feet into the floor, hitting back at him and reaching nothing but air. Sadie couldn't dislodge the man's hand to scream.

Then she realized Barnaby wouldn't hear her anyway, because he was in the woods burying the man's accomplice, so she went limp. Her captor had to double his efforts to get her out of the tent, but once out, he held a gun to her side.

"Call out or make any sound and you die right here, right now." A growly voice whispered. "Followed by the wounded man and then that mountain of a man you showed up with. Understand?"

Chills ran up and down her spine at the thought of the man killing Barnaby and her baby. She nodded.

"I'm removing my hand, don't forget. One sound is all it takes."

Even though he'd told her not to, she considered screaming for Barnaby. But she would only get herself and her baby killed. She couldn't allow that to happen.

He removed his hand.

She said nothing. Not a single sound...just to be safe. She looked back at the tent and knew Seth couldn't help her. She just hoped he didn't die before Barnaby returned. Sadie needed for Seth to tell Barnaby what happened.

The man forced her to bend over. Then he did the same, as though by getting lower, Barnaby wouldn't see them. He walked her into the forest, careful to keep his pistol trained on her.

She was sure she would die or he would rape her, or both. Sadie would rather die than be raped. If Barnaby would just come out of the forest now, she would be saved. But he didn't.

When they stepped through some trees and into the forest, he straightened.

Sadie did the same, still looking at the place straight behind their claim. But she saw nothing, no movement of any kind. She knew the trees were thick and, even if he'd been returning, he most likely wouldn't see them because he wasn't looking for them. They would already be too far in to be seen from the river.

The man sidled in behind her.

She'd noticed before that he was only about an inch or two taller than she was. He wore grubby wool pants and a wool flannel shirt that was the standard for miners to wear. From the stench, it was clear he'd never washed his clothes. She'd decided from his dirty hair and beard, it had been a lengthy time, if ever, since he'd taken a bath.

He poked her in the back with the barrel of his gun. "Move. We've got a long way to go, and I don't want to get caught out here at night."

She didn't either, so she picked up her pace, wondering if it wouldn't be better to be devoured by wild animals than what he undoubtedly had in mind. She walked farther and farther away from the man she loved. Away from Barnaby.

* * *

BARNABY RETURNED to the camp after burying the dead man. He went to his claim first and, not finding Sadie, he set out for Seth's property.

He looked around inside the tent, but he only found Seth on his cot.

Barnaby shook him. "Where's Sadie?"

Seth groaned. "Took her. Couldn't stop him. Claim jumpers." Then he fell silent.

Sadie. It was probably Homer who had Sadie. He looked up and prayed. "Please don't let them hurt her." Bending over his friend, he checked Seth's pulse. It was, strong and even. Closing his eyes, he thanked God that Seth's wound wasn't as serious as he thought it would be.

He stood and gently slapped Seth's face. "Seth. Seth. Wake up. Where's Sadie? Seth, please wake up."

He slowly opened his eyes, widened them, and stared at Barnaby. "He took her. He took her."

"Who? Who took her?"

"Claim jumper. Friend of Grimes. Said they would make her pay for shooting Homer."

Barnaby stood and cursed under his breath. "Seth, I have to leave and you have to stay here until I come back. I don't want you wandering around and dropping dead somewhere because you started bleeding again. It's nearly stopped, but if you move around much, it'll start again. I'd stitch you up but I have to find Sadie first."

"I understand." He gripped Barnaby's arm. "Go. Find her before they hurt her."

"I plan on it." He turned, stepped out of the tent and looked at the muddy ground. The marks of where she'd been dragged out made him want to hurt someone. Following the drag marks, he saw where they stopped and she'd regained her feet. Then her captor walked behind her. She wouldn't have gone willingly. Not with her expecting. She would have done everything to stay alive and keep their baby safe. He suspected she might even love him, but those thoughts had no place in what he'd do today...after he found her. Whoever took her had just poked the sleeping bear.

CHAPTER 11

With the sun at her back, Sadie walked through the trees in front of the man. The trees weren't as thick in this part of the forest and if he didn't have a gun on her, she would've run. But she couldn't take the chance of him shooting her.

"Where are you taking me?"

"Never you mind. Just keep walkin' until I say stop."

Sadie huffed out a breath and didn't care if he knew she was angry. She had every right to be.

She looked around her, searching for a landmark she'd be able to find when she fled. Escaping was definitely when, not if, because she had to get back to Barnaby. What if she was never to tell him she loved him? She didn't want to die without him knowing.

They walked until they reached a clearing. In the middle was a tent and a man hobbling around a fire.

Grimes. Homer Grimes. She'd know that limping cretin anywhere.

As they approached, Grimes stopped and turned toward them. "Well, if it isn't Mrs. Drake. Don't think you can shoot me this time. Matter of fact, you can't do anything about what I'll do to you."

Even with the gun pressed on her back, she'd never felt fear like she did now. She was afraid she was utterly at his mercy, and he had none of that particular trait in him.

He limped toward her until he was only two feet away.

"You know Barnaby will kill you for taking me. The only chance you have of living is to let me go. Then I'll tell him. I'll plead your case and say it was all a big mistake."

Grimes paused at her words and then backhanded her.

She fell to the ground. Her nose felt like he broke it again, but her entire face throbbed, so she wasn't sure.

"He ain't comin'. He don't even know where you are."

She stood and wiped her split lip; a swath of blood now covered the back of her hand. "He'll track you. He's good at that, so good he never comes home empty-handed when he hunts. You're a dead man Homer." She turned toward the man who brought her. "And so are you. Dead men."

"I...I don't know, Homer. Maybe she's right. That Barnaby is a big man. Even if we get him by surprise, it'll take both of us to put him down and you being crippled and all won't be much use. I say we take her money and run."

"Shut up, Monty. We'll get her money and something else on the side. How long's it been since you had a woman? Huh? We got one now, and I mean to take advantage of the situation."

Sadie laughed; the sound maniacal to her ears. "I'll die before I let you take me. Then if you had any hope of living, it's gone. He'll kill you on sight. It won't matter where you are. You'll be dead. Hiding in town won't save you."

Homer's eyes abruptly shifted to something behind her.

She turned around to see Barnaby entering the clearing. She smiled and looked at Homer over her shoulder. "I hope you're prepared to die because you are soon to meet the maker, and God is not about to be happy with you. But Satan will welcome you with open arms, and may you rot there."

Barnaby fired his pistol.

Monty went down, gun still in his hand.

Homer grabbed Sadie around the throat with his arm and shoved a pistol in her side. He stared over her shoulder at Barnaby.

If she was certain she wouldn't get shot, she'd send her elbow into his diaphragm. But the way he was holding the shaking gun, she couldn't risk it. Couldn't risk the baby.

"Don't come any closer, or I'll shoot her. She'll die

before you get her to a doctor. Just like your friend, Seth."

Barnaby stopped in his tracks. "The only one dying this day is you. You shoot my wife, and I'll make sure you writhe in agony. You let her go, and I might give you a chance to shoot me first. Your choice, Grimes."

The more Sadie focused on her husband, the more she respected and loved him. He was amazing. Calm and cool. Nothing Grimes said made any difference to Barnaby. Grimes had seen fit to kidnap Sadie this time, and Barnaby would not be forgiving. He had his chance to live when her husband hadn't tracked him down last time. But now, he had no chance. She knew that, but Grimes didn't, or he thought he could beat Barnaby. But that wouldn't happen. Her man was good; slow, methodical, accurate. He didn't waste ammunition, not while hunting and not while facing down a criminal like Homer Grimes.

Suddenly, Grimes pushed her away and fired his pistol at Barnaby.

Barnaby hadn't moved, but now he took aim and fired. The bullet hit Homer in the middle of his forehead.

She'd known Barnaby was good from when he was teaching her to shoot, but that had been practice. Now was real life, and he'd just saved hers. She took off running toward him. When she reached him she launched herself at him, knowing he would catch her. He would always catch her. She wrapped her long legs around his waist and her arms around his neck. Then she peppered his face with kisses before he stopped her.

"That's no way to kiss your husband, the man who just saved your life, now, is it?"

As tears filled her eyes, she laughed. He'd saved her from a fate worse than death. Though she was prepared to fight, their advantage in numbers was too great. She knew the men could have overpowered her and taken her.

Tears rolled down her cheeks, and she buried her face in his neck.

He rubbed her back with one hand and held her to him with the other. "Here now, *mo grah*. You're fine. I wouldn't have let anything happen to you. You're my wife. No one takes what is mine."

Sadie realized he didn't say he loved her. Did he? What about their baby? Would he love him? She'd already decided she was having a boy. Someone big and strong as his father. Someone who wouldn't have to marry just to be safe on her own property. She unwrapped her arms from around his neck and put them around his shoulders. "You can let me down now."

He held her as she lowered her legs from his waist.

She stood. "We should probably head home."

"We have to bury these men, or the animals will carry parts of their bodies all over the forest. No one wants to be walking and run into human bones."

"Of course, you're right. I don't know what I was thinking." *I was thinking we should just let the buzzards and other scavengers take them, but that would be an unChristian thing to do. I feel bad even thinking such a thing, but Homer Grimes was evil, and Monty was just as bad since he's the one who actually kidnapped me.*

Barnaby searched the camp for a shovel and found one. He started digging; the ground having thawed enough to make his task possible.

A couple of hours later, he had the hole as deep as he could go before the ground became too hard.

He pulled himself out and carried both men over and dumped them in the hole. Then he covered it with the dirt he'd dug up.

After he was done, he used the clean water in the bucket by the fire to wash the dirt from his face and hands. His clothes were filthy and would have to be scrubbed sooner than she'd planned.

What would she do if he didn't change his mind? If he didn't love their child? She would never raise a child with a father who didn't love him. She couldn't subject any child of hers to that heartache. Better to never have a father at all.

She was quiet on the walk home.

"Sadie, are you all right? I don't think you've said a single word since we started back to camp."

"Sorry, just thinking."

"What is it that has you contemplating so hard?"

She thought quickly. "I was just thinking about Seth. I wonder if he's all right. I didn't have time to tend his wound."

"He'll be fine. No need to worry about Sam. He's been in worse situations and come out just fine."

She looked up at him. "How would you know? Did you know him from before?"

"Yes. He's my friend. We've known each other since the California gold fields."

She stopped, put her hands on her hips and narrowed her eyes. "But why haven't I known this? We should have had him over for dinner after you went hunting. I'm sure he would have appreciated it, and his presence would have added to our conversations."

He started to touch her and then looked down at his clothes and stopped. "It wasn't something I was keeping from you. I just didn't think about it. We talked occasionally, and that was all we needed."

She shook her head and started walking again. "Men!" Stopping abruptly, she turned toward him. "Did you ever think I might need a friend up here? You're my husband, but I could still use a friend, man or woman. But since I'm the only woman around here, it would have to be a man."

Barnaby growled and took her by the upper arm. "You'll have no man friends."

Sadie slowly curved her lips into a smile. She was aware he was restraining his strength, for he wasn't hurting her in the least, just stopping her from walking away. "You're jealous."

"I'm not. I'm just your husband. You shouldn't need any other man."

"I'm not proposing that I have relations with him,

just that I can visit him if I want, especially if you're off hunting. I'll feel safer knowing I have someone I can count on."

He released her. "Well...I suppose that makes sense. We'll stop and see him on the way home anyway, and see how he is. He might need some doctoring."

"And I want to thank him. He was wounded because he helped me."

They started walking again and came to Seth's camp first. It was quiet.

Then Sadie heard a moan from in the tent.

"Barnaby. Seth."

"I heard it." He rushed and opened the tent flap. "Seth. Seth. Talk to me. It's Barnaby."

The man opened his eyes. They were bright with fever.

Barnaby looked over at Sadie. "I'll get some water from the river. You light the stove and start that bucket heating."

She had already started for the stove. Wood and kindling were stacked neatly next to the wall of the tent. Sadie built a fire and put the half-full bucket of water on the stove.

Then she looked for clean washcloths but didn't see any.

He had a metal locker under his cot. She opened it. There, folded neatly, were washcloths, towels, a couple of shirts, a pair of long johns, several pair of wool socks and a pair of wool pants.

She grabbed out the washcloths and then pulled his shirt all the way open.

Barnaby returned with the bucket of icy river water and set it on the floor near the flap.

"I need your help with his shirt. The wound must be cleaned."

"Earlier, I checked him and found out the bullet had passed through his body. Therefore, he requires the front and back cleaned and then sewn shut."

"I can stitch him up if you'll hold him after I get the dirt and blood cleaned away." She dipped one washcloth into the heated water and scrubbed at the wound below his left ribs until the blood that oozed out was clean and red. Then she did the same with the back wound.

She found a sewing kit in the metal locker. She had Barnaby hold him still while she stitched up both wounds. Then she rinsed a clean washcloth in the icy water and wiped down Seth's chest, arms, neck and face.

Through all of this, Seth remained blissfully unconscious.

"One of us should be with him all night, in case he wakes up. Do you have more of that willow bark?"

Barnaby nodded. "I do, and I can make more."

She bathed his forehead. "That would probably be a good idea. We need to keep it on hand at all times. Which shift do you want?"

"Neither, we stay together. He's got enough room on the floor for one of the mattresses. We can share it.

You'll just have to sleep on top of me." His mouth quirked up on one side and he winked. "You usually do anyway."

Her face heated, and she smiled. "Yeah, I guess I do. Okay, I'll stay with him and keep rubbing him down with cold water to see if his fever will break. You can get the mattress and bedding."

"On my way." He stepped out of the tent.

She turned her attention back to the injured man on the cot. "Thank you, Seth. You stopped that claim jumper and we're grateful, so don't you go dying on me before we get to thank you properly."

Barnaby came back with the mattress and then left again for the blankets.

After he returned, she made the bed while he worked to cool Seth's heated body. After a couple of hours of being rubbed down, Seth started to shiver. The fever broke, and now he had the chills.

"So...so...cold." Seth's teeth chattered.

"I'm just glad you're awake, my friend." Barnaby took his hand.

"Yes, we might have given up and left you for dead. Just kidding," said Sadie.

Seth chuckled. "Ow, ow, don't make me laugh."

"You'll be fine, you old faker," said Barnaby.

"Perhaps, but why would I want to stop having a beautiful woman fuss over me?" Seth grinned.

Sadie slapped the washcloth against his shoulder. "We're staying here until we think you can get on by yourself."

"I'm fine. You two don't have to worry about me." He braced himself on the edge of the cot, threw his legs over the side and sat up. "See? I'm a tough old bird. Ain't that right, Barnaby?"

"That you are, but we'll be staying a few days to make sure."

"If you must." Then he grinned. "I'm looking forward to some good cooking."

Sadie pulled a slow smile. "I can't say how good the food will be, but I'm sure we'll do our best. I do breakfast and breads. Barnaby does lunch and supper."

"Any cooking that's not mine is very much appreciated. I need to get up and do my business. Barnaby, will you help me get on my shirt and then out there?" He pointed outside.

"Sure." He helped Seth button his long johns and then put on his shirt. "Just lean on me and I'll get you there."

Sadie watched as the two men left the tent. She had a new friend, and she couldn't be more pleased, except if Barnaby would tell her he was happy about the baby. That worried her most of all.

CHAPTER 12

With Seth's recovery going well enough for them to return to their own camp, Sadie and Barnaby started working the river again.

Sadie worked up river from her husband when she noticed a small spring emptying into the river. She went to it, reached down into the hole the water bubbled from. She brought up a handful of dirt and rocks. Only when she got them in her pan, she saw they weren't rocks, but nuggets.

Oh, my God. Her heart pumped and her body felt like lighting was running through it. She had to show Barnaby. She stepped out of the river and ran down to him.

"Barnaby! Barnaby!" she called over the roar of the river.

He looked up from where he stood about twenty feet from her, with his legs apart and braced against the rushing water.

She waved him over.

"What is it you need that couldn't wait?"

She opened her hand.

His eyes widened as he took in the large nuggets she held. "Where did you get these?"

"Out of a spring just up the way." She pointed to where she'd come from. "It's on our claim. I made sure."

"Show me." He walked to the tent and grabbed a shovel.

She led him to the spring.

He took the shovel and dug down into the bubbling water. He brought up a spade of dirt and put it into her pan.

She added water and worked the pan. Nuggets appeared quickly, and gold flakes with them.

He spaded more and more dirt into her pan. Finally, he dug back toward the forest to see where the gold was coming from. He pointed out a good-sized crack in the dirt and saw his dream. A vein of pure gold ore. Barnaby dug as fast as he could. The vein gave them nuggets and flake for days. His bag and hers were both full. He got another one from his supplies and, in just a couple of days, filled it up.

They needed to go to Dawson City to get the gold weighed and exchanged for cash. But they couldn't leave the claim empty.

"You go to Dawson City tomorrow." Sadie spooned a savory chunk of venison from her chili. "We could use some supplies while you're at it. As far as me here, it won't be any different from when you go hunting.

You can have Seth keep an eye out for me. Ask him to dinner tomorrow night when you get back with some potatoes and carrots, if you can find them. We still have some elk chunks left and I'm sure he would again appreciate a meal other than his own cooking."

Barnaby sopped up the last of his dinner from his bowl with sourdough bread. "That should work. You know, as soon as word gets around town about our find, we'll have desperate men following me here. We'll have to be even more vigilant than normal to keep what is ours."

"I know, but we don't know how long the vein will last and it's not really that big."

"Big enough to make us rich, I'd say."

"I hope you're right. What do you want to do with your money?"

"I want to buy a ranch and raise horses, maybe some cattle. What about you? What do you want to do with the money?"

"I'd like to get what we can get and then get out of this godforsaken place and back to civilization. I desire a gracious home where we can raise our child with comfort and safety.

A smile traversed his lips. "Are you saying you don't love our little bit of heaven here?"

She came close to spitting out her food, but she chewed and swallowed. "Heaven? Have you lost your mind? We're only doing this for as long as it takes for that vein to play out. When it does, I'm out of here."

The smile left his face. "You'll stay as long as I do.

You're expecting my child, and I won't have you endangering him by gallivanting over the countryside."

Her gaze slammed into his, anger radiating through her. "This is a child you don't even want. Don't suddenly decide you can tell me what to do with *my* child."

"I'll tell you whatever I darn well please and whether or not I want this child, he is still mine and I take care of what's mine."

"So do I." She shoved up from the table. "I need to do the dishes." She put the water on to heat and walked out of the tent to get another bucket of water. *Dang men. Where does he get off telling me what to do with my child? It would be different if he wanted him, but he doesn't, and he shouldn't get to choose what I do.* She reached down and rubbed her belly, which was now rounded with her baby. "Don't you worry, little one, I won't let anything happen to you."

As she approached the river, she heard Barnaby coming up behind her.

"Here, let me get that." He took the bucket and waded out to the deeper water so it would be clean. He walked back to dry ground and up to the tent.

She followed, muttering under her breath. "I'll tell him what he can do with his rules. I will take care of my baby."

After the dishes were done, she stripped down and crawled under the blankets.

Barnaby followed suit, blew out the lantern and

then tugged her back against his chest. "I don't enjoy arguing."

"I don't like it either." She kept her back to him.

He rubbed her shoulder and down her arm. "Talk to me, Sadie. What's really the problem?"

Tears prickled in her eyes. "You should be happy about the baby, and it kills me you're not. This child is a part of us and we both should love it."

"Things can always change. I might feel differently when the baby is here, I don't know. I'll tell you I'm scared, Sadie. I don't want to go through the pain of losing another child."

For such a big, scary man to admit such a thing, touched her in a way he never had before. She rotated to face him, although the darkness prevented them from seeing each other. "I'm scared, too. I've never had a child to love. Someone who will depend totally on me for his life, now and after he's born. It's scary. What if I do something wrong?" She reached up and found his face, cupped his jaw and lifted herself to kiss him. First, she kissed his chin, but she eventually found his lips. "Light the lantern. I want to see you. I want to show you and have you feel me."

He turned away, found the matches, and lit the lantern. He kept the flame low, so it cast the tent with pale light and shadows.

Sadie lay on her back. She took his hand and placed it over her belly. "This is us. Our child, who we made together. This is a miracle. We created life. Someone who is the best of both of us, who we can teach to be better than we are."

Barnaby closed his eyes. "What if he dies? What if he never gets the chance to—"

She placed two fingers against his lips. "Shh. I'm not your first wife. I'm not sick. I'm healthy as a horse. Our child will be healthy and strong, just as you are and I am. And, by the time this little one is born, we'll be rich and can take care of him, regardless of what happens. I believe that. I have to believe that."

"You make me want to believe."

"Then do. Try to picture us together, growing old and watching our children grow and marry and give us grandchildren. That's the way it will be. Trust me...trust us. We might not love each other, but we can love this child we created." *How can I tell him I love him without scaring him away? Better to let him think we don't love each other. I don't want him to say the words if he doesn't mean them, or because he thinks that is what I want to hear, even though it is.*

"I'll do my best, but I can't promise something that I'm not sure will happen."

"All I ask is that you try."

He turned, aligned his body with hers, and when his lips were a whisper away from hers, he stopped. "I'll do my best." Then he kissed her.

She wrapped her arms around his neck and let the love she had for him go. Let it surround them. She had enough for both of them...for now. His kiss deepened, and she felt like lightning was shooting through her to her core. She pulled back, but kept her arms around his neck. "Make love to me, Barnaby. Now. Make love to me now."

"With pleasure, *mo grah*. With pleasure."

He passionately kissed her again, and then he made love to her. She savored every moment as though they had all the time in the world. The time and place faded, leaving only the two of them together. His movements were not frenzied. He adored her entire body tenderly and then he covered her, leaving her content, fulfilled, and hopeful. Surely he had to love her. He couldn't make love to her like he did without loving her...could he?

The next day after breakfast, Barnaby headed to Dawson City and Sadie went back to the strike and dug and dug. The vein was going deeper and Barnaby would have to do the digging, but she hoped that wasn't the end. She only thought of it after he left, but she hoped he came back telling her he'd opened a bank account and deposited the money. He would be in great danger of being bushwhacked if he carried all the money back with him. Many desperate men had turned to crime when their claims turned out to be devoid of gold.

Barnaby and her father were lucky to have gotten one that was paying out.

She stood, placed her hands on her hips, and then stretched her back.

Her back had been paining her more than usual, and she couldn't determine if the pregnancy caused it.

She was only about five months pregnant, and if her body was this sore now, what would it be like when she was nine months along?

Sadie looked over toward Seth's claim.

He was working the river but saw her and waved.

She waved back. He was a good man, and she hoped that someday soon he would have a wife who was worthy of him.

Shading her eyes, she looked up at the sun. Barnaby had been gone for hours and should already be on his way back. Her stomach rumbled, and she realized she'd skipped eating lunch. It was time for a break and she needed to eat and she was definitely hungry now.

Picking up the shovel, she headed back to the tent. She had the rest of the morning's loaf of bread and the last of the huckleberry jam from their previous trip to town. She hoped Barnaby would bring more home with him. She hadn't asked, and it was probably out of stock, but maybe she'd get lucky.

She realized she was too tired to go digging right after eating, so she lay down for a quick nap.

Sadie awoke to Barnaby shaking her shoulder.

"Sadie. Sadie. Wake up."

"Barnaby? What are you doing back so fast?"

"Sweetheart, it's after five in the evening. I'm actually back later than anticipated. How long have you been sleeping?"

She sat up, yawned and scratched her head. "I laid down after lunch. I thought I'd only take a quick nap. Apparently, my body said otherwise."

He smiled, bent down and gave her a tender kiss. "You must have needed it. You can't be working so hard in your condition."

"I have to. The harder we work, the sooner we can get out of here."

He sat back on his haunches. "We've made a bunch of money. The gold ended up weighing more than I thought it would."

Her eyes shot wide. "I knew we had a lot in those bags I've almost filled another one, just today. That vein is solid."

"I know. I bought some dynamite. We can cut it into smaller charges and break up the vein."

"That would make it a lot easier to get to the ore."

"My thoughts exactly. I want you to stay in the tent when I'm using it. You don't need dirt and rocks raining down on you."

"You don't either."

"I'll be out of harm's way, but the dynamite is dangerous stuff, and I want you safe."

She thought that was incredibly sweet. *Maybe he has some feelings for me, after all.*

"Okay. I'll stay here. Then, after you're done, I can help you with the panning. Now I need to get up. I have to add to my sourdough starter so I can bake tomorrow. If I don't do it now, I'll forget, and it's already almost too late." She got out of bed and went to the shelves on the other side of the woodpile next to the stove.

"I'll start dinner. I got some more potatoes and carrots while in town." He grinned.

"Why are you grinning?"

"You haven't asked how much gold we had in those big bags."

She stopped, jerked around and put her hands on her hips. "Well, are you going to tell me, or do I have to guess?"

He stood, walked to the table, and sat. "Guess."

"Well, those were the twenty-five pound sugar sacks and none of them were full. I'd guess eighteen pounds of gold each. Am I close?"

He nodded. "Yes, you are. There were one-hundred-fifty-two plus pounds in total. I opened a bank account in both our names at the Dawson City Bank. I deposited fifty-thousand dollars and kept out two-hundred and change. That will keep us in whatever supplies we need for a while."

She walked to him, sat on his lap, and then wrapped her arms around his neck. "We're rich and I bet we get more than that out of the vein after you dynamite it. I bet I took at least fifteen pounds out of it today."

"I'm thinking that if the vein plays out, we still have enough to go somewhere, buy a house and live where it's not frozen all the time."

"We aren't frozen now. We're muddy now. Is this the way summer always is? Muddy?"

"We've had some drier days, but now that it's September, we'll start getting the first snows. They'll be light and melt quickly, but the days will be much colder."

"I can tell already." She stood and pulled one of Barnaby's wool sweaters from his cot over her head, glad for the extra room. It accommodated her expanding middle nicely.

Barnaby stared at her.

"What are you looking at? You appear as though you've never seen me before and you can be sure that you have."

"No, I don't think I have. Looking at you now and seeing your belly expanding with our child has shaken something loose inside me. I don't want you working in the creek any longer."

She put her hands on her hips. "That's ridiculous. I'm still quite capable of doing my share."

He looked up as she sat back on his lap. "Sadie, I don't want you to hurt yourself or this child." Barnaby placed his hand gently on her stomach.

She covered his hand with both of hers. "I would never do that. I want this child more than anything. If it came down to perhaps hurting him, I'll leave the gold and take my child out of here."

"Let's see what's revealed from the dynamite and decide then."

"Agreed. Will you do that tomorrow?"

"Yes, the sooner, the better. Snow will be here before you know it, and we can't leave then. The trek is too dangerous."

"It was bad enough in the end of March. I wasn't

sure I'd get here." She thought of all she would have missed if she hadn't been able to complete the journey, and it saddened her. "But thanks to the tram, I made it. We came to an accord and created a child. I wouldn't trade that for anything."

"Nor would I. But now, I must get to dinner. You need to keep your strength up. You're eating for two now."

She frowned. "I wish he would stop pressing on my stomach. It might actually make it easier to eat for one."

Barnaby chuckled. "Ornery already. I can tell he's my son."

She tilted her head. "Were you full of mischief when you were young?"

"Yes, I was. My mother used to curse me. She was just a little thing like you." He grinned. "Well, she was tall like you, anyway. But I was almost this height when I was twelve. I added a few inches, but I've been this tall since I was about fifteen. I was so much bigger than her that when she cursed me, I just picked her up, swung her around, and gave her a kiss on the cheek. She was laughing by the time I was done and couldn't remember why she'd cursed me."

Sadie chuckled and by the time he finished his story, she was laughing. "Your poor mother. I don't know what I'll do if this one is like you. I need an easy first child so I can learn to be an exemplary mother." She lifted her chin a little. "And I will be."

He cupped her jaw and ran a thumb over her cheek. "I don't doubt it. You can do anything you set your mind to. You're the strongest and most determined woman I've ever met."

He lowered his head and gave her the tenderest kiss he'd ever given her.

She aligned her body with his and kissed him passionately, playing and loving him as much as he allowed. If only he knew the extent of her ardor, maybe he would let go of his own feelings and love her back. Maybe. Was she wishing for something that could never happen?

CHAPTER 13

The next day, under a sunny sky, Barnaby dug the holes and set the charges.

When they exploded, Sadie couldn't help the small scream that escaped. She heard the rocks and dirt hit the tent and was glad Barnaby had insisted she stay inside.

Now, though, she ran out to make sure he was okay. When she got to him, he was grinning like a fool.

"What? Are you all right?"

"I am. Look at the ground. What do you see?"

She looked and saw it littered with nuggets, large and small, of pure gold. They glinted and glittered in the morning sun. She turned around grinning, her body tingling. Her father would have been so happy.

"What about the vein? Does it go farther?"

He shook his head. "Unfortunately, no. The last charge didn't show any sign of a gold vein."

She waved at the ground. "Well, let's get this picked up and then be gone from this place."

"We can't leave until we're sure."

"Yes, we can. Leave the claim to Seth. He can get whatever remains."

He set his jaw, hands on his hips. "No. We're not leaving."

Sadie couldn't understand his sudden greed. "We have what we came for. By the looks of it, we'll have as much, or more, gold when we're done here than you took back to Dawson City yesterday."

He lifted his gaze skyward and raised a fist high. He walked in a circle, as though he could calm himself that way. "That's not the point. I've lived up here for two years now. No one wants to go home more than I do, but I won't leave until I'm sure we've gotten all we can get. John and I made a pact."

She fisted her hands and put them on her hips, her breath so tight in her throat she could barely speak. "A pact with a dead man is more important than what your wife needs?"

Barnaby lowered his hand, released his fist, and turned toward her. "In this instance...yes."

"Then I'll go by myself."

Barnaby walked toward her, stopping less than a foot away. "You'll do no such thing. It's too dangerous."

She didn't back up but stiffened her spine. She took her fisted hands and held her arms straight at her sides. "I came by myself and I can get home by myself."

Barnaby gritted his teeth and hissed out a breath. "You will be the death of me."

"Then come with me." She hated to beg for anything, but how could they have a life together if he didn't come and she wasn't having her baby in some dirty backwater mining town. "We have enough to start a new life...together. Where do you want to live? What do you want to do? We've got enough money to do it. You want a ranch, right? We can do that. Or just a house somewhere. We can do any of that. Why can't you see...it's enough?"

"Your father understood. I lost my wife and son chasing after this." He bent and picked up a good-sized nugget off the ground. "Now, I've found it. I can say losing them wasn't in vain."

She understood now. She would never be enough. Their children would never stand up against the baby he lost. "I'm glad to know where I stand...where my child stands." She turned and walked into the tent.

If she left now, she would make Dawson City by mid-afternoon. She pulled out her pack and filled it with clothes. That was all she would take. She'd get money when she hit town and she still had fifty dollars left from the cash she'd brought with her. She was entitled to half of what was in the bank. Perhaps not legally, but he'd said they would split it evenly and he'd set the account up in both their names. She'd take her half, have most of it wired to her bank in St. Louis. She still had an account there. Maybe she knew she'd be returning, just not alone.

* * *

BARNABY GRITTED HIS TEETH. His stomach turned somersaults because he knew he couldn't do or say anything that would make Sadie stay. The only thing he could do was let her go. He walked over to Sam's camp.

"Sam, can you escort Sadie to Dawson City? She's not having anything to do with me right now and is, in fact, refusing to talk to me. I have some gold to pay you for your trouble." He held out two nuggets the size of chicken's eggs.

Seth's eyes widened. "I thought when I heard the blasts from your claim this morning that you must have hit something. But I didn't expect this." He took the nuggets. "I'll see her safe to Dawson City and into the first group heading back."

"Thank you. She can be very stubborn, and I don't really blame her. Winter's coming and it's best if she isn't here, though I can't tell her that now."

Sam waved a hand and frowned. "Why not? Is it better to leave things left unsaid when the words could heal the wounds that are bound to fester?"

Barnaby paused and considered his friend's words. "You're a smart man. Tell me again why you haven't taken a wife?"

Seth shrugged. "Maybe when I go back to civilization, I'll think about searching for a wife."

"I'm trusting you to take care of mine."

"Consider it done."

Seth went into his tent, got his coat and stuffed

some clothes in an old flour sack before returning to Barnaby.

"Where is she?"

"She already took off on the horse. She said I could carry the gold on my back since it was so important to me."

"Did you hit the big one?" Seth's eyes widened.

Barnaby saw excitement twinkle in them. "We hit a small vein. The dynamite looks to have uncovered the rest of it we haven't dug up yet. I'll be here collecting the nuggets on the ground and then doing a bit of digging to make sure we got all of it."

"Then you'll go after her?"

He looked in the direction she took, sadness almost overwhelming him. "Yeah, I'll go after her."

Seth clasped a hand on Barnaby's upper arm. "You didn't tell her, did you?"

Barnaby looked away. "Tell her what?"

Seth grabbed him by his shirt and turned him back. "Look at me. This is Seth you're talking to. I've known you too long. You don't get to play dumb with me. You didn't tell her you love her. She might have stayed if you had."

"If she loved me, she would have stayed." His throat felt clogged, and he swallowed over a lump the size of one of those nuggets he'd just given Sam.

"Why? She wasn't getting anything from you in return. Why should she have stayed? And why are you sending me after her when you could go yourself?"

"I can't go. There's a lot of gold here to be collected.

It could take me a week or more. She couldn't stay even that long."

"Again, why should she? She's got a child to take care of. If she doesn't go now, she might be stuck for the winter. You don't want that baby born here. Do you?"

Barnaby huffed out a breath and ran a hand through his hair, his other on his hip. He walked in a circle, trying to figure out what to do. "No. I don't want the baby born here. The little mite will have a hard enough time of it without trying to survive in the freezing winter."

"Barnaby. Look at me. What is the right thing to do? What is more important—the gold, or your wife?"

As if lightning had struck, he knew what to do. "Sam, will you deal with the claim? You can keep half of what you pick up and all of what you dig up. I trust you and know you'll be fair. I have to go after my wife. She's been gone too long. I don't know if I can catch her before Dawson City."

"Then I guess you'd better get moving. I'll collect everything I can and bring it to you as soon as possible. My claim isn't paying out anything and it sounds like yours is played out now, too."

"Yes, I believe it is, but we did well. And from the looks of all this." He swung his arm wide, "you'll do well, too." He walked to his friend and hugged him. "Thank you, Sam." He released him and hurried back to his camp. He was taking only what he needed in his pack. He was about to leave when he noticed a glint of gold on the table, along with a piece of paper.

Since gold is what you love, here is the last bit for you.

The wedding ring he'd purchased her on their second night in the honeymoon suite, was on the table.

He picked up the ring and put it in his pants pocket. He set off after his wife. *What have I done?*

* * *

SADIE GALLOPED when she could and walked Lucky the rest of the way to Dawson City. She made good time, arriving in the early afternoon. She headed straight to the bank.

When she walked in, Reginald Whitmore, the bank president came out of his office and greeted her.

"Mrs. Drake. I hadn't expected to see you so soon." He looked around the bank lobby. "Where's Barnaby?"

"He's still at camp. He'll be meeting me later, but seeing as I'm expecting, we don't want to get caught by the winter and have the baby here or God forbid, at the claim."

"Very understandable. What can I do for you?"

"I'd like you to wire half the money, less five-hundred dollars to this account in St. Louis. Barnaby will get the other half when he comes through later on."

"Well, this is most unusual, but Barnaby did set up the account in both of your names and made sure that I knew you had access to any and all of it."

Sadie's throat clogged at the thoughtfulness he'd given to setting up the account. She was sure that Reginald wouldn't have given her the money without that stipulation. "Thank you. I have to see about catching the next riverboat out of here. You'll excuse me if I ask for a receipt, please."

"Of course." He wrote her a receipt for twenty-five-thousand dollars and handed it to her. "I wish you the best, Sadie...may I call you Sadie."

"Please, do."

He extended his hand. "I hope you have a happy life."

Tears filled her eyes but she smiled. "I'm sure we will. Thank you."

Then she headed to the riverboat station.

She walked into the building and up to the counter. "I'd like one ticket for Skagway."

"You're in luck. We're just loading up and getting ready to leave. That'll be one-hundred dollars just to Skagway, assuming you don't take the tram, but if you can afford it, I recommend the tram. It will save you weeks and harsh conditions that walking over Chilkoot Pass will dish out. You'll have to get a steamer from Skagway." He turned his gaze toward the gray sky. "Looks like you're getting out just in the nick of time. Winter is on its way."

"I know, and I don't want to spend winter here. The summer has been long enough for me. How long will it take to get to Skagway without the tram?"

"It might be a little shorter as the pass is easier to

cross this time of year, but it's two months more or less. If you take the tram, you'll shave two weeks off that for sure. I'm glad to see you're prepared for the weather."

"I understand." Sadie paid her money and walked over to the group that was getting ready to load into the boats to travel upriver. She'd take the tram again. No reason to walk over the pass. Then she'd walk down to Skagway.

She'd hoped Barnaby would come after her, but now she looked behind her and wondered if she'd ever see Barnaby again.

* * *

BARNABY ARRIVED in Dawson City in the late afternoon. He headed straight to the ferry station. He approached the man behind the counter. "When is the next trip to Skagway?"

"Well, hi Barnaby. We just had one leave today. Might be next week or next month. Depends on the ferry captains."

Barnaby wanted to drag the man over the counter by his lapels but restrained himself. "Can you tell me if a woman was in the group that left today?"

"Funny you should ask. There was one. The last passenger in the group. Came to the counter just as we were loading up."

Barnaby cursed. She'd made better time than he thought she would, but she was on horseback, after all.

"Send me a message at Kitty's when you know the departure date of the next boat." He placed a five-dollar bill on the counter.

The clerk snatched the five and tucked it into his pants pocket. "Sure thing. I know Kitty's. I'll let you know."

"Thanks." He took off toward the assay office. He wanted a hot bath, but that would have to wait. First, he needed to cash in this gold, then head to the bank and find out what, if anything, Sadie had left him.

The gold he'd brought amounted to twelve-thousand-six-hundred-and-twenty-seven dollars. He hoped that the remaining gold would yield at least as much for Sam. He'd talked Barnaby into coming after Sadie; otherwise, he might not have found her for months. At least, now he had a chance. Maybe.

When he walked into the bank, the manager, Reginald Whitmore, greeted him. Reginald was a dapper man wearing a three-piece suit and tie. Not something anyone saw much of in Dawson City. Most of the men were like him, wearing mining clothes, wool everything—pants, shirt, and socks.

"Barnaby. I wondered when you'd be in. I hadn't expected you today, though. Sadie was here just a few hours ago, and I thought she'd left you on the claim."

"She did...until I came to my senses and followed her. But I wasn't fast enough. She got on the last ferry."

Reginald turned toward the back. "Come to my office and we'll talk." He walked to his office, waited until Barnaby had entered, and then closed the door after him. Then he made his way around the desk. "Have a seat, please." He pointed at the straight-backed wooden chair in front of the desk as he sat in the large leather chair on the other side. "Hopefully, there will be another ferry soon. But what can I do for you today?"

Barnaby sat forward in the chair. "I want to close the account. I know I just opened it a few days ago, but I have to go after her."

"Ah, I understand. She left you approximately one-half of the money. Do you have an account you want it sent to? Or will you be using the same account as Mrs. Drake?"

"I want it sent here." He handed him a piece of paper with the name and account number of his bank in San Francisco. "All but five-hundred dollars. I'll need that to see to my passage and my room at Kitty's, plus food until I can get passage. And we both know that could be days or weeks or months."

"That's true. I'll wire the rest to your bank first thing in the morning. It's too late today."

"That's fine." He stood and extended his right hand toward the bank manager. "I'll be staying at Kitty's if you need me."

"I believe I have everything I need. If you'll wait a few minutes, I can get you a receipt for the transaction."

"Did Sadie send her half to a bank in St. Louis?"

"Yes, the First National Bank of St. Louis."

"Thank you. I appreciate your assistance."

"Anytime. Do you think you'll be back?"

Barnaby shook his head. "Not in this lifetime." He accepted the receipt. Then he left and headed toward Kitty's and the bath he promised himself.

Though Chilkoot Pass was travelable all year round, in winter, it was more treacherous. He was glad Sadie would get out before then and hopefully she'd be able to take the tram.

He walked into the hotel and met Kitty behind the registration desk.

She looked up. "Barnaby." Kitty leaned to the side, trying to peer around him. "Where is Sadie?"

"She left earlier today for Skagway."

Kitty tilted her head. "Then what are you doing here?"

Barnaby sighed. He needed someone to talk to, so he told her what had happened.

She lifted a brow and leaned forward, resting her forearms on the desk. "I'm glad you realized your mistake sooner rather than later. Hopefully, you'll get a ferry soon and might catch her in Skagway."

"I'm hoping, but no matter where she goes, I'll find her. I can't let her go. She's my wife and I love her."

She cocked an eyebrow. "Too bad you didn't tell her that before."

He looked toward the ceiling, hoping to get an answer and knowing he wouldn't "I know. I was a fool. But I'll make it up to her as soon as I find her. I'll show her I'm a changed man, if she'll just have me back."

"I wish you luck. The only room I have open is that honeymoon suite that you've had before."

"That's fine. I'll need a bath, too."

"I'll send one right over. Just sign here." She turned the register toward him.

He signed the book, took the key, and headed back to the room. Inside, he set his pack on the bed, then sat on the edge of the mattress, rested his elbows on his knees, and placed his head in his hands. "Sadie, what have I done? I'm so sorry. I hope you'll forgive me." Tears formed and as he sat there, he felt them roll hot and fast from his eyes.

"Please forgive me."

CHAPTER 14

*S*adie arrived in St. Louis exhausted. The morning sickness, first on the steamer and then on the train, had nearly drained her. She needed to buy clothes. She'd gotten some in Seattle and then again in Chicago, but she was growing faster than her wardrobe would allow. She also knew before any of that she needed to see Angus Murphy and see if he could find her a place to live. She didn't want to stay in a hotel for any longer than necessary, but, at least, being back in civilization, she could get back to her frugal ways. She still had enough cash to rent a room in a nice, average hotel.

Angus' secretary looked up when Sadie walked in.

"Miss Thompson. We didn't expect you. I thought you were in the Klondike."

"I was, but I completed my business there, so I'm back. Is Mr. Murphy in? I really need to talk to him."

The gray-haired woman smiled. "He's always in for you. Have a seat, and I'll check with him."

Sadie perched on the edge of the leather chair. She didn't want to sink down and have trouble getting up. Being almost eight months pregnant, certain things were more challenging now, getting up from soft sofas and chairs being just one of them.

Angus Murphy walked out of his office. "Sadie. How are you, my dear?"

She tried to stand with as much grace as possible.

"Here dear, let me help you." He held out his hand.

She took it and let him pull her up. "Thank you. I'm good. Glad to be back home. I have to admit, that was one of the hardest things I've ever done."

He looked down at her belly. "But it looks like it might have also been one of the most rewarding."

She placed her hand on top of her protruding stomach. "Yes. When I got there, I was informed the only way I could go to the claim was to marry Barnaby. I agreed. So, we married and eventually, I found myself pregnant."

"Come into my office and you can tell me all of it and how I can be of service." He held out his arm.

She placed her hand in the crook of his elbow, and they proceeded to his office.

He assisted her into a chair and then went around and took his own chair. "Can I have Clara get you something to drink? Some water? Coffee? Tea?"

"A cup of tea would be lovely. I don't believe I've had a decent cup of tea since I left."

"Certainly. I'll be right back." He left the office.

While he was gone, Sadie wondered how much to tell him. He was a good family friend, but she didn't want to burden him with her problems. Still, he was sort of like her uncle and he was her father's best friend. She needed someone to talk to and decided she would tell him everything.

Angus returned with a cup and saucer. "Here you are, my dear. Now, tell me how I can be of assistance."

Sadie explained everything that had happened since she'd left. She took a sip of her tea. "Oh, my, this is lovely. Anyway, now that I'm back here to stay, I'd like to find a home to purchase. I want a nice place to raise my child."

He leaned back in his chair and steepled his fingers. "As it so happens, I still have your home available. I never sold it. I thought, perhaps, you might come back. If you hadn't after a year, then I was going to sell it. It's exactly as you left it, if you are interested."

Sadie burst into tears. "Oh, my God. You don't know how happy I am to hear you say that. My home is the perfect place to raise my baby. Thank you. Thank you so much."

He stood and came close, handing her his handkerchief. "There, there now. All will be well. I'm sure your husband is on the way to you as we speak. He probably just missed you. You'll be reunited soon, I'm sure."

The thought of not seeing Barnaby was too real. Her chest ached when she thought about it, and yet she didn't believe he would come for her. He didn't love her. "I'm not. What if he never comes?"

"That isn't something you should be worried about. You have a baby to think about. I'm sure you need to purchase things for yourself and for the little one on the way. Clothes. Furniture. So many things that a new little child will need."

"You're right. I need to concentrate on the baby, for now. Barnaby can do whatever he pleases. I intend to raise my child alone."

"What do you need of me, besides the deed to your home?"

"I'd like for you to become my man of business, just as you were for my father. I have over twenty-thousand dollars that needs to be invested and managed. Less the money you gave me for the house. But you always did so well with my father's and with my money that I'd like for you to continue."

"I'd be happy to. I'll have the papers drawn up and bring them over myself." He reached into his top right-hand drawer and withdrew an envelope. "Here are the keys to your home. I'm sure you'd like to spend the night in your own bed."

Her eyes teared. "Yes, I would like that more than anything. Thank you. Thank you so much for this. It's the best gift I've ever received."

He walked over to her, handed her the envelope and patted her hand. "You're welcome. I'm glad it has worked out this way."

Levering against the chairs arms, she stood. Sadie

kissed his cheek. "You are such a dear man. Thank you."

His color rose. "Anytime. Anything for John Thompson's daughter."

She left the office and took a Hansom cab to her home. Her steps were light as she walked up to the door. She removed the key out of the envelope and a note fell out.

My dear Sadie,

I never wanted to sell your home. Your father would have haunted me all my days if I'd left you homeless. All the clothing and furnishings you left behind are still here and haven't been sold.

I hope you will enjoy being back in your grandmother's home and that she and your father keep a watch out for you.

Your friend,

Angus Murphy

Tears filled her vision, and she wiped them away with the palms of her hands. She turned her face skyward. "Thanks, Daddy, and you, too, Gran, for watching out for me. Now, if you can let Barnaby find me, I'd be most grateful."

She took the key and stuck it in the door. The mechanism turned flawlessly and the door swung wide.

Picking up her duffle, she stepped up into the foyer with its white marble floor and delicate chandelier. The signs of luxury her grandmother had insisted on when she'd had the house built were even more beautiful after so long in the Yukon Territory. But one thing the house didn't have was Barnaby. Would she ever see him again? Would he come after her?

She sighed as she ascended the carpeted stairs which led up to the bedrooms. She took her bag up to the master bedroom. That had always been her parents' and even after her father left, she'd never felt right about moving in there. Now, they were both gone, and she was the mistress of the large house, about to have a baby. She couldn't stay anywhere else since they had attached the nursery to the master bedroom.

She headed to the kitchen to see if there was anything to eat, but the cupboards and icebox were empty, as she expected. Since it was early afternoon, she had time to go to the market. The house was only about four blocks from there, so she could easily walk the distance.

An hour later, she walked up the path to the front door and let herself in again. Carrying the bags of groceries wasn't easy. Thankfully, she was in good shape because of the heavy physical labor she'd done working the gold claim. She carried the groceries to the kitchen and put the teakettle on. A nice cup of tea would be lovely.

By the time she'd put all the groceries away, the kettle was whistling. She measured one-half-teaspoon of tea into the bottom of a cup and poured the water over the leaves. She found the matching saucer and set the cup on the table.

A knock sounded at the front door.

She opened it and saw Mrs. Underwood, her old

cook. With her hair as white as snow and her little round spectacles, she was a friendly face, which Sadie realized she needed more than anything.

"Well, if you aren't a sight for sore eyes." She folded Sadie into a tight hug.

"Won't you come in and have a cup of tea with me?"

"I'd love one."

Sadie led the way to the kitchen, where she got another cup and saucer. She prepared the tea the same way as she had for herself. When finished, she carried it to the table and set it in front of the woman. "Here you go." She sat across from the cook. "How did you know I was back in town?"

"Mrs. White, down at the market, said she'd seen you and that you were back to stay." She lifted her eyebrows and leaned forward. "Is that true? You're here to stay?"

Sadie smiled and nodded. "I am. I want my baby to be born here." Looking down, she rested her arm on the top of her belly.

"It's a good house to grow up in, as you well know."

"I do. I'm looking for staff for the house. Can you recommend people?"

"Well, there's me—"

Sadie's eyes widened. "You're available? I didn't dare hope. Of course, you. You're hired. Your bedroom is off the kitchen—" She stopped and laughed. "Of course, you know that. I also need two maids and either a cook or a housekeeper, depending on which position you would like."

Mrs. Underwood took a sip of tea. "Oh, I'll be staying the cook. I don't want the headaches that can come with being the housekeeper. But I can get the other positions filled if you'll trust my judgement."

"Of course. You've been the cook here since I was a child. I trust you implicitly."

"Good, I'll be by tomorrow with the women. Now, I need to go and inform them of their new employment."

Sadie walked her to the door and gave her a hug. "Thank you for stopping by. You've just made my life a lot easier."

With her staff in place, Sadie felt she could rest now. She was so tired; it seemed like all the time she felt like she needed a nap. She knew it must be the baby, but she was tired of feeling tired.

The next day, bright and early, Mrs. Underwood returned with the three women who would now work for Sadie. She greeted each woman and then put them to work cleaning the house, which had sat empty for nearly a year.

She was ready for the baby and nothing could go wrong now.

* * *

A KNOCK SOUNDED at the front door.

Alice, the downstairs maid, answered it.

Sadie was on a ladder dusting the top of the book-cases in the study.

"What in Hades are you doing, woman?"

Sadie whipped around. Her heart pounded like it was trying to escape her body. "Barnaby?"

He rushed up and caught her as she lost her balance and fell.

She wrapped an arm around his neck. "What are you doing here?"

"I came to find my wife, and when I do, she's trying to kill herself climbing ladders she has no business being on."

She liked being held safe in his arms, but she wasn't about to tell him that. "You can put me down now."

He shook his head. "I don't think so. I like you right where you are."

She stared up at his face. "You do?"

"Yeah. I do."

Sadie sighed and melted into his powerful arms. He cradled her gently like she was a small child and he might break her. "I missed you."

"I was a fool. Choosing gold rather than the treasure I had right in front of me. I love you, Sadie Drake. Do you forgive me?" He carried her over to the brocade sofa that faced the bookshelves she was working on and sat with her on his lap.

Tears welled up in her eyes. "Oh, Barnaby. I love you, too. I shouldn't have left."

He pressed a finger against her lips. "Shh, *mo grah*. You were right. I gave the claim to Seth. I hope it proves to be as good to him as it was to us. I left almost immediately after you did. Seth pointed out what a fool I was, and I realized he was right. But you'd already left

185

on the ferry. I had to wait for nearly a month to follow you. I was afraid I would miss the birth of our child." He ran a palm over her belly. "I want this child, more than you can imagine. He's a part of both of us, and I want him. And I want you. Please don't send me away."

She cupped his beloved face. "Never, my love. Never." She waved an arm, taking in the room. "This was my childhood home."

He followed her arm and looked around the room. "How did you manage to buy it back?"

"Angus never sold it. He said he would have if I wasn't back in a year."

"I'm glad you got it back. John wouldn't have been pleased if you raised his grandchild anywhere but here."

"I admit, I had a pretty glorious life here. Even though it was my grandmother's home, Dad never minded. He knew I'd inherit the home eventually and wanted that for me."

"I'm glad." He looked down at their hands together on her belly. "You look like you're ready to have this baby, but I see something missing from your hand." He reached in the inner pocket of his jacket and pulled out her wedding band. "Hold out your hand. I don't want to release you. Will you, Sadie Drake, be my wife and the mother to all of our children, starting with this one?" He leaned over and kissed her belly.

She laughed. "I will, if you will promise to love me forever."

"That's easy, I already do." He took her lips with his and kissed her like she'd wanted him to for months.

Suddenly, Sadie felt something wet between her legs. "Mayhap sooner rather than later. I think my water just broke."

He swiftly stood. "Then let's get you to the doctor."

CHAPTER 15

"We need a Hansom cab. You can send Clara for the doctor. She's my cook and my friend. She's in the kitchen. That way." Sadie pointed down the hall.

"There's Hansom cab outside. I asked him to wait since I didn't know what kind of reception I would receive." He ran down to the kitchen.

A few minutes later, he and Clara returned.

She ran outside to the waiting Hansom cab.

He carried Sadie from the study upstairs. "What room is yours?"

"The first one on the left."

Barnaby opened the door and set her on the floor by the bed. Then he turned down the covers and lifted her, settling her in the middle of the bed.

"Ahh. Darn that hurts." After a minute or so the pain subsided. "Dr. Wilcox is on Second and Market. It will take Clara a while to return with him. I need to get into my nightgown."

"Where is it?"

She pointed toward the bureau with the attached mirror. Bottom drawer in the middle.

He retrieved the ratty nightgown and held it up. "This one? It looks like it's about to fall apart."

"It's the oldest one I have. I don't want to get a better one messed up like this one will be after the birth."

"Ah, I understand." He took the gown to her and helped her into it.

About half-an-hour later, the doctor arrived with Clara.

Doctor Wilcox was an older man. He'd been her doctor since she was a child. His hair was white now, but he still looked the same to her.

Barnaby greeted the doctor. "I'm Barnaby Drake. My wife's having a baby."

"Calm down, young man." The doctor chuckled. "I didn't think you called me here for tea." He turned her gaze toward Sadie. "Well, hi, Sadie. Ready for that little one to get here?"

"Oh, yes, Doctor. More than ready. This hurts so much."

"Don't worry about it. You won't remember a thing when he gets here, except what a beautiful baby you're having. Trust me."

Sadie huffed out a breath. "I'm trying. I'm truly trying to take this in stride."

He looked at Barnaby. "I've been waiting to meet you. I'm Jason Wilcox. You must be Barnaby Drake." He extended his hand.

"I am and I'm glad to meet you, too." He held Sadie's hand with his left and put the right out to take the doctor's hand.

The doctor turned to Clara. "We'll need hot water and towels to clean the baby and Sadie afterward."

Clara nodded. "I'll go get the water started. And I'll bring a bucket of cold so we can make it whatever temperature you need." She rushed from the room.

"Good. Is there soap over with the pitcher and basin on the bureau?"

"Yes, Doctor, it's filled with fresh water every day," said Sadie.

Doctor Wilcox nodded and set his doctor's bag on the bureau, opened it and took out his instruments. Then he turned back to Sadie. "I have to ask a couple of questions first. Now, Sadie, when did your water break?"

"About thirty minutes ago."

"And the contractions? How many have you had in that time?"

"I don't know. It seems constant. Four, maybe five, I guess."

The doctor smiled. "Well, that's a bit fast for them, but first babies can come quick. Let's look, shall we?"

Barnaby stood next to the bed and held Sadie's hand.

"I need to examine her. You can wait downstairs.

Afterward, if she's not already delivering, you can come back. I feel sure that it will take some time for her to deliver, so you two can visit until then."

Barnaby shook his head. "I'd rather stay. I know it's not traditional, but I don't want to leave her in her hour of need." He looked down at Sadie. "I already did that once and I never will again."

She squeezed his hand and smiled.

The doctor raised his brows. "Well, that is most unconventional, but if you stay at her head, it should be fine. Let's take a look and see where we are." He turned his attention to Sadie. "Lift your knees and spread them apart, please. You know what to do."

Sadie did as he asked.

By this time, Clara had returned.

"Clara," said the doctor. "I need light."

She grabbed a lamp off the nightstand and held it for the doctor.

"Well, I'll be." The doctor's brows lifted and his eyes widened. "You are delivering right now, Sadie. I need you to bear down as hard as you can. Push. Hard. Harder. Don't stop until I tell you."

Sadie snagged Barnaby's hand and squeezed it as hard as possible. Her belly grew rock hard and she gritted her teeth. "Ahh." She stopped. "I can't do it anymore. I need a break."

"That's fine," said Dr. Wilcox. He glanced down. "Break's over. Bear down. Hard. Come on now, I know you can push harder."

Sadie didn't know how long she pushed and

stopped, then pushed again. Finally, she felt the baby slide from her body. "Is he here?"

The doctor chuckled. "Yes, your *daughter* is here."

"A girl." She turned her face up toward Barnaby. "Did you hear? We have a daughter." Tears chased one another down her cheeks, and she didn't care. She had her baby and her husband.

"I see, my love. A daughter." He caressed Sadie's face and kissed her forehead.

Clara took the baby to a table across from the foot of the bed. She cleaned her up and then brought the swaddled infant to her mother.

Sadie lifted her arms, eager for the baby to be in them. When Clara laid the baby in her waiting arms, she brought her to her chest.

"Here love, I'll sit behind you and you can sit up and lean on me."

"Yes, that would be perfect."

He lifted her to a sitting position and then sat behind her, acting as her pillows.

She laid the baby in her lap and unwrapped her. "She's beautiful. Perfect."

The baby girl stared up at Sadie when she talked.

"That's right, little one. You're perfect, and your daddy and I love you very much."

Barnaby reached over Sadie and gently spread his hand on the baby's head. "She's so small. My son was never this small. He weighed ten pounds when he was born. I didn't think my wife would speak to me ever again." He turned toward the nurse. "How big is she?"

"She's seven-and-a-half pounds and twenty-one inches long. She's going to be a tall one."

"Well, her daddy and I are not small." Sadie laughed. Then she looked up at her husband. "What are we going to name her?"

He pulled on his chin like he had a goatee and was pulling it to a point. "I've been thinking about that. What do you think about Riley? I know it's unusual, but it's an old family name. Or maybe we could use it as a middle name. Would you like that better?"

"I like that. I was thinking about naming her after my mother.

What do you think about Grace Riley Drake?"

"I think it's beautiful, just like she is." He put a finger in Grace's hand.

Grace clamped her tiny fingers over his big one.

Sadie watched him as the changes overcame him. Wonder. Awe. And finally, pure love.

The doctor came over to them, wiping his hands on a towel. "I want you to stay in bed for a full week. Then you can get up, but you must take it easy. I don't want you to do anything strenuous."

"That won't be a problem, Doctor. I'll see to it," said Barnaby.

Sadie could hardly take her gaze off Grace but she managed it. "Thank you, Dr. Wilcox. I think I would like to be home with my daughter and my husband."

"That's a good idea. I'll come by in a few days to see how you're doing."

"Doctor, will you hold Gracie while Clara and I help Sadie get dressed?" asked Barnaby.

The doctor beamed. "I would love to."

Barnaby eased the baby out of Sadie's arms and passed her to the doctor. Then he helped Sadie into a new, pristine white nightgown.

Clara whisked away the dirty bedding and oilcloth, then put down a fresh sheet.

When she was ready, Sadie took the baby back.

Barnaby scooped both of them into his arms and laid them in the center of the bed. Then he sat on the bed with them.

"Why don't you lie down next to me?" Sadie asked.

He sat on the bed with his back against the headboard and stretched his long legs. He leaned down and kissed her. Then he leaned forward a little and kissed Gracie on the forehead. "My two girls. I love you both more than I can express." He lifted Sadie's head with a knuckle under her chin. "Thank you for taking me back and giving me the most wonderful gift I could ever get. A beautiful baby girl to love and spoil."

"You can't spoil her yet. I fully believe that babies can't be spoiled. You cannot spoil her by holding her too much, kissing her too much, or loving her too much."

"Looking at my child now, I'd have to agree with you." He stopped and gazed at Sadie. "I'm so glad you came into my life."

"So am I. I took a chance to find adventure and feel alive, and I found love instead. I never expected you or that I'd love you. But I do. You gave me this most precious gift. Gracie." She looked down at the baby in her arms. "She's everything to me. I would give my life for either of you."

"As would I."

"Let's put her down and then I'll let you hold me until we sleep."

"Nothing would give me greater pleasure."

She reached up and stroked his face, now covered in a heavy beard. Then looked again at their daughter, who was now fast asleep. *How did I get so lucky?*

"I ask myself the same question."

"I didn't realize I said it out loud." She grinned. "Or do you now read my mind?" She tied on a new cloth to catch her blood and hopefully, keep the sheets clean.

Barnaby undressed as well.

They both got into bed and she snuggled into his arms as though no time had passed between them.

Sadie laid an arm on his chest and tangled her fingers with the soft curly chest hair. "I missed this."

He tucked her even closer. "As did I."

Sadie looked up at him. "I don't think I've had a truly good night's sleep since I left you."

"Nor I, since you left."

She settled; her body completely relaxed. She yawned.

"I love you. Thank you for finding me."

"I love you back. I would have kept searching for the rest of my life. I don't have a life if you're not in it. Now, sleep, my love. I have you."

Sadie yawned again. Her family was now complete. A tiredness swept over her like someone had lifted a weight replaced by a deep contentedness. And it had. She no longer had to face a life alone. She had her husband and daughter to love and love her back.

All was finally right with the world.

EPILOGUE

*T*hree years later

SADIE SAT on the back porch swing holding her eight-month-old son, Jamie, in her arms.

The baby stood bouncing on her lap as they watched his sister and father playing in the yard.

Gracie would run, and Barnaby would give chase until he caught her, usually in just two steps. Then he'd grasp her under the arms and swing her high in the air. All the while, she giggled.

Barnaby walked onto the porch, carrying his wiggling daughter under one arm. She was turning three that day.

Laughing, Sadie leaned to the right and looked at her upside-down daughter. "Gracie, what do you want for your birthday?"

"A sisser or a puppy."

Sadie chuckled. "A sister or a puppy, huh. Are they the same in importance, or would you rather have one more than the other?"

"Puppy." She wiggled around. "Down, Daddy."

"Sure thing, *ah storeen*, my little treasure." He turned her and set her on her feet. "There you go, sweetie."

She wobbled a little before finding her equilibrium. Then she shot off the porch, her long red braids swinging back and forth as she ran to go play with her dolly, who lay dejected on the lawn.

"A sister or a puppy, hm?" asked Barnaby. "I know my preference." He waggled his brows.

"Oh, quit, you silly man. You know we'll have to find her a puppy now. She doesn't want to wait another six months to possibly give her a sister. After all, the baby could be a boy, which will not make her happy."

Jamie started fussing and leaned against her chest.

"Oh, are you a hungry boy? Hm?" She opened her bodice and set him to her breast. "Barnaby?"

He stood there, wide-eyed and shoulders slack. "Six months? You're expecting again?"

Smiling, she nodded. "I am. I was going to tell you tonight, but Gracie's wish was a good way, too. Are you all right?"

He sat on the swing next to her. "Another baby." Barnaby turned with a grin. "You know how much I love babies and children. This is a wonderful surprise." He leaned over and kissed her.

Jamie pushed at him with his little hand.

She reached down and smoothed Jamie's brown hair. It was the color of his father's but with her wild curls. Unlike Gracie's which was as red as a sunset and straight as a doornail. Neither one would be happy with their hair when they were older. It was just the way of things. "It would seem that your son doesn't like to share."

Barnaby laughed. "It would seem so, wouldn't it?" Reaching down, he wrapped the baby's hand around his thumb and then smoothed an index finger over Jamie's fingers.

Jamie looked up at his father and grinned without ever letting Sadie's nipple slip from his mouth.

Babies were talented that way.

"Are you ready to add another baby to this group? You'll have two in diapers."

She sighed. "Hopefully not for long. I'm trying to potty train Jamie before the next one arrives. You can bet he won't want to when she gets here. He'll want more attention and could regress to needing a diaper, but at least he'll know what to do."

"However you want to work it, my love. I'm behind you. I'll always support whatever decision you make regarding our children."

She leaned over and rested her head on his shoulder. "I know, and I appreciate it."

He looked down at Jamie. "It appears he was more tired than hungry."

"So it would seem." She buttoned her blouse, picked up the baby into her arms and then stood. After she burped him, she headed into the house. She stopped and turned to Barnaby. "Get her inside fairly soon. After I put him in his crib, I'll have Clara prepare supper."

He stood with her. "I've got her. Don't you worry."

She tipped back her head, waiting for a kiss.

He obliged. Holding her gently so as not to crush the baby and wake him up, he kissed her thoroughly.

She pulled back. "If I didn't have Jamie, I'd kiss you back properly and then we'd set on the swing and pretend we're still in the Klondike, just the two of us."

"I don't have to pretend. Whenever I'm with you, it's just the two of us. You are my sun and my moon. You and these children are everything to me. You are my life."

"And you are mine. I love you, Barnaby Drake."

He grinned, reached up and cupped her face. "I love you, Sadie Drake. Forever."

"Forever isn't nearly long enough, but I guess it will have to do."

He called to Gracie. "Come on, *ah storeen,* my little sweetheart. Time to go in."

"Do I get mik and cookies?"

"What do you say, Mama, one cookie?" asked Barnaby.

Sadie shook her head. "She really shouldn't. Dinner will be in about an hour."

"She's like her daddy. We'll be starving by then."

Laughing, Sadie placed her head on his chest. "You two are peas in a pod."

He wrapped an arm around her shoulders as they walked inside to their own little world.

ABOUT THE AUTHOR

Cynthia Woolf is a USA Today Bestselling Author and an award-winning author of sixty-five historical western romance novels, two time-travel western romance novels, five contemporary western romance novels and six sci-fi romance novels, which she calls westerns in space.

Along with these books she has also published nine boxed sets of her books. The Tame Series, Destiny in Deadwood, The Marshals Mail Order Brides, The Brides of the Oregon Trail series, Centauri Series and Swords and Blasters.

Cynthia loves writing and reading romance. Her first western romance Tame A Wild Heart was inspired by the story her mother told her of meeting Cynthia's father on a ranch in Creede, Colorado. Although Tame A Wild Heart takes place in Creede that is the only similarity between the stories. Her father was a cowboy, not a bounty hunter, and her mother was a nursemaid (called a nanny now), not the owner of the ranch.

Cynthia credits her wonderfully supportive husband Jim and her great critique partners for saving her sanity and allowing her to explore her creativity.

STAY CONNECTED!

Newsletter
Want to hear about coming books first?
Sign up for my <u>newsletter</u> and get a free book.

Follow Cynthia

https://facebook.com/CynthiaWoolf
https://twitter.com/CynthiaWoolf
http://cynthiawoolf.com

Don't forget if you love the book, I'd appreciate it if you could leave a review at the retailer you purchased the book from.
Thanks so much,
Cynthia

ALSO BY CYNTHIA WOOLF

The Brides of the Klondike
The Gold Rush Bride

* * *

The Prescott Brides
A Bride for Ross (Available in German)
A Bride for Frank (Available in German)
A Bride for Tucker (Available in German)
A Bride for Clay (Available in German)
A Bride for Brodie (Available in German)

* * *

Billionaire Cowboys
Her Secret Cowboy Billionaire (Available in German)
Her Mysterious Cowboy Billionaire (Available in German)
Her Royal Cowboy Billionaire (Available in German)
Her Bachelor Cowboy Billionaire (Available in German)
Her Christmas Cowboy Billionaire (Available in German

* * *

* * *

The Marshal's Mail Order Brides (Available in German)

The Carson City Bride

The Virginia City Bride

The Silver City Bride

The Eureka City Bride

* * *

Bride of Nevada

Genevieve

* * *

Brides of the Oregon Trail

Hannah **(Available in German)**

Lydia **(Available in German)**

Bella **(Available in German)**

Eliza **(Available in German)**

Rebecca **(Available in German)**

Charlotte **(Available in German)**

Amanda **(Available in German)**

Emma Rose **(Available in German)**

Nora **(Available in German)**

Opal

* * *

Brides of San Francisco (Available in German)

Nellie

Annie

Cora

Sophia

Amelia

Violet

* * *

Brides of Seattle (Available in German)

Mail Order Mystery

Mail Order Mayhem

Mail Order Mix-Up

Mail Order Moonlight

Mail Order Melody

* * *

Brides of Tombstone (Available in German)

Mail Order Outlaw

Mail Order Doctor

Mail Order Baron

Central City Brides (Available in German)

The Dancing Bride

The Sapphire Bride

The Irish Bride

The Pretender Bride

* * *

Destiny in Deadwood (Available in German)

Jake

Liam

Zach

* * *

Hope's Crossing (Available in German)

The Stolen Bride

The Hunter Bride

The Replacement Bride

The Unexpected Bride

* * *

Matchmaker & Co Series (Available in German)

Capital Bride

Heiress Bride

Fiery Bride

Colorado Bride

Troubled Bride

* * *

The Surprise Brides

Gideon

* * *

Tame (Available in German)

Tame a Wild Heart

Tame a Wild Wind

Tame a Wild Bride

Tame A Honeymoon Heart

Tame Boxset

* * *

Centauri Series (SciFi Romance)

Centauri Dawn

Centauri Twilight

Centauri Midnight

* * *

The Swords of Gregory (SciFi Romance)

Jenala

Riza

Honora

* * *

Singles

Sweetwater Springs Christmas

Made in United States
Troutdale, OR
07/13/2024

21198151R00126